W9-CUC-053

Fifteen Rabbits

Fifteen Rabbits
A celebration of life by
Felix Salten

Translated by Whittaker Chambers
Illustrated by John Freas

DELACORTE PRESS/ELEANOR FRIEDE

Designed by Ann Spinelli

Library of Congress Cataloging in Publication Data

Salten, Felix, 1869–1945.
Fifteen rabbits.

Translation of Fünfzehn Hasen.
I. Freas, John.   II.   Title.
PZ3.S1733Fi7   [PT2637.A52]   833'.9'12   75–35808
ISBN: 0–440–02563–X

*If you would keep men from
becoming as animals, strive
ever to see animals as men.*

Fifteen Rabbits

"Where are my brothers and sisters?" The little rabbit, who was sitting beside his mother under the fern-fronds, suddenly asked the question.

He was no bigger than a lump of earth from the forest loam. He looked like a ball of wool, but he seemed almost as soft as the softest down, almost as light as air. He was quite covered with a misty-gray color of that fine mixture which we call pepper and salt. He was as insubstantial, and at the same time as wonderful, as the first pale shimmer of the early morning that was just breaking. On his brow was a white star, the emblem of his childhood.

"Where are my brothers and sisters?" he asked
again. He had just remembered them, he did not
know why; and he did not bother his head about it.
He was accustomed to asking questions, therefore
he asked.

His mother was silent.

A large and stately hare, she sat cowering low on
her haunches. She had a black stripe at the bend of
her spoonlike ears. Her powerful white whiskers
kept up a gentle but constant motion. It seemed impossible that the tiny youngster beside her would
ever become as large as she was.

"It seems to me," he began again, "it seems to me
as if I had several brothers and sisters."

As no reply was forthcoming he continued,
"Brothers and sisters were with me. But I don't know
how many of them now; it was so long ago, and I
was still too small, at that time."

That "long ago" and "at that time" had their own
meaning, for the little rabbit had been in the world
only a few weeks.

1

Without changing her position, his mother turned toward him very slightly. But her whiskers moved somewhat more energetically. "Yes, yes!" she said, "you're getting bigger, Hops, my dear. It's really astonishing how fast you're growing."

The diminutive Hops reared himself up straight, sat on his hind-legs, raised his ears delightedly. "Where are the others?" he insisted.

"Disappeared," his mother answered softly.

The small ears flattened. "You disappear sometimes, too," he said, "but you come back again."

His mother kept her nose pressed between her fore-paws and was silent.

Hops suspected something bad. "When . . . will the others come back again?"

His mother pressed her head still closer between her fore-paws and answered even more softly, "Never."

"Where are they?" Hops was anxious, but he did not give way to it.

"They are lost."

Hops did not quite understand what he heard. But he was alarmed. After a pause he asked, "And I . . . will I be lost, too?"

His mother trembled. "Hops . . . my beloved Hops . . ." She sighed before she continued, "You must take care, must watch out constantly, constantly. Constantly—do you understand? And you must be able to run quickly, quicker than any other creature in the forest."

"Oh, but mother," Hops solemnly affirmed, "I always do watch out. I don't even know exactly why, but I do watch out."

"You're a good boy," his mother praised him. "Some day you'll learn for yourself why we must always be on guard. You're still my little one."

"And I can run, too," Hops exclaimed, "just watch me!"

He began to run, awkwardly, childishly, but with the best of wills. He bounced around his mother, scampering in wider and wider circles.

His mother sat still and watched him. A brief sense of satisfaction warmed her heart. Then she muttered to herself, "One way or another . . . no one can hold one's children . . ." She let her stately ears droop mournfully and slowly as she repeated the words, "One way or another . . . our children never stay with us . . . there comes a day when they need us no more."

Hops fell into an ecstasy of running. That little ball of gray wool, as Hops' mother called him, bounded over the ground, under the fern-fronds and lettuce leaves, under the low thin branches of young dogwoods and blackberries. Many of the stalks brushed him softly as they flew back. It was pleasant; it made him want to run still faster.

The forest began to awaken.

A pale light filtered into the thicket through the fresh green of the tree-tops.

With a loud rustle the pheasants left their roosts, and their metallic calls, splintered and bursting, rang out everywhere. They sounded as though tongues of dazzling flame were flaring up here and there throughout the forest, only to die out again. They sounded like cries regretted even at the very moment of utterance, cries of mingled pain and desire.

High overhead, on the highest, thinnest, topmost branches of the beeches and lindens sat the blackbirds. Seen from the earth they were no bigger than black specks, but the May morning was alive with the haunting and changeable music of their songs.

The oriole's golden-yellow body darted from tree to tree and exulted as it flew, always with the same inspired notes, as if the sun had just risen.

The angry screaming of the jays shrilled through the air. The dancing, laughing tones in which the magpies chatter could be heard. The bushes were alive with the delicate twittering of the brisk little titmice and the chirping of the hedge-sparrows.

Again and again, from far and near, the cuckoos called.

When Hops came back after his run, his mother was gone.

He did not look for her.

Several other young rabbits came through the underbrush. Here and there, quite close sometimes, sometimes farther off, they bounced and ran or sat erect, their ears pricked up.

Hops, who knew them all, joined their revels.

2

Hops spent many other morning hours out on the meadow with the companions of his childhood.

During the long, wondrously varied hour of the waning of night, when the darkness lifted and floated off like a black veil, as the sky grew brighter and the stars paled, during that hour the little rabbits frolicked on the meadow.

It lay in the midst of the leafy forest and had no exact shape, either circular or otherwise. In one place the forest flung out an advanced spur like a narrow peninsula. In another place the meadow dug a bay deep into the thicket. Only a lake, a pond, or a wild meadow could be so irregular, so fascinating. It was like a breathing-space in the huge forest, a little spot of freedom, light, air and—danger.

There the young rabbits romped about in the happy frenzy of childhood.

They resembled little wisps of clouds still bearing the light of the sky in them. They looked so disembodied, so soft.

Round and round they chased one another, close to the edge of the forest. Then a Something, always present to their childish senses, told them one can never know what may happen, and that it was to their advantage to vanish with one bound into the thicket.

Hops was one of the most cautious of them. Often he would feel an urge to run farther and farther into the middle of the meadow. He restrained himself, now and again with an effort, though he did not know why. He always remained quite close to the thicket, ever prepared to flee and hide himself.

Little Plana entrusted herself to his guidance. It had come about quite by chance.

Plana was lively and wanton, though without the least self-consciousness.

When the others rolled head over heels because they scampered so fast, little Plana was in the thick of it. When they all bounded into the air, transported by their own involuntary somersaults, and first really began to run as though bewitched, Plana was the maddest among them.

Then Hops would wiggle his ears and call to her. "Plana!"

She came at once.

"Stay with me."

She stayed. She sat beside him, gazing happily at him. He kept silent.

She was charming, that little Plana. There was something touching about her, some quality of helpless devotion.

Hops could not understand it so clearly. But he felt it well enough when Plana was sitting beside him.

Sometimes the little rabbits were almost crazy with joy in themselves, in the strong, enlivening morning air, in the breath of the grasses and flowers.

Then they would bounce one after the other so swiftly that it was impossible to tell which was the pursuer and which the pursued. They couldn't have told themselves.

Plana, too, fell regularly into that ecstasy which even Hops could not withstand. He romped with Plana, back and forth, up and down, but always near the thicket, always close to the protecting bushes.

If Plana wanted to dash wantonly over the meadow, Hops would instantly recollect himself and call, "Not so far!"

Plana would come back and sit down beside him, merely saying, "You're always afraid."

Haughty pheasants strutted across the grass, brilliantly colored, proud, with nodding heads. They were the fathers of families on a holiday. Inside, in the more open thicket, the hens were leading about their broods. The mothers, swarmed about by the little chicks, had a downcast, self-conscious air and could never sit quietly because of their constant watchfulness.

Out on the meadow a deer would lift its head, move its ears gracefully and stare at the playful little rabbits.

Sometimes they lost their breath, running and jumping. Then they would sit still, assume serious, even grave, expressions. At such moments the shadow of a hard destiny to come seemed to lie upon them all.

Without stirring they would sit while their chests heaved and their pulses throbbed.

But such young rabbits do not take long to recover themselves.

Soon one would begin again, sit up on his hind-legs, peer impudently around. A second would hop up to him and nudge his flank. A third would act as if the whole flock were after him and run like mad.

Then the whole band would begin running at once in circles.

One day, however, the general happiness was seriously disturbed.

One diminutive little rabbit was so out of his senses with joy that he kept on running, right out into the middle of the meadow. He was a gay little thing, the maddest, the liveliest of them all. Confident, curious, inexperienced, befuddled by his own joy, he kept on running.

A pair of crows, who were sweeping over the field, saw the little rabbit bouncing alone across the meadow.

The black birds swooped quickly down upon him, and, before the poor thing could think, he felt a burning pain in both eyes. The beautiful green world vanished, grew black. Agony shot through his brain. It was all over.

The cry of the dying young one who had hardly

begun to live passed unheard. Too softly it sounded, too suddenly it ended.

Nothing was left but some scattered bits of soft wool and a little blood that clung in ruby-red drops to the grass-stems or soon soaked into the earth.

Several of the little rabbits had not even noticed the incident. A few had seen the crows swoop down. During the brief moment that they sat erect with their ears lifted, they had guessed rather than witnessed the death overtaking their comrade on the meadow.

Perturbed, they dropped down and fled in the midst of their game, into the thicket.

But not one of them said so much as a word to any of the others about what had happened.

A silent horror possessed them, diminished in time but made them untalkative.

Hops was sitting under a low, thick eldershrub on the edge of the meadow, with Plana beside him. Above the elder and the other bushes towered a huge and ancient oak, its branches spreading gloriously.

Two squirrels chased one another up the tree and down again. Their red plumes twitched among the bright green leaves.

"It's dangerous to run out like that . . ." Hops said softly.

Plana merely sighed.

They both sat quite still. Now and again their ears moved, their whiskers quivered.

When the sun rose and its first rays blazed down like far-flung, golden spears, the little rabbits crept into the cool shade of the thicket. They did not remain together. Each of them slipped off to the bed he had hollowed out under the overhanging branches of some bush. Everyone alone and everyone for himself, their thin little bodies nestled into the warm earth, they lay without motion and gave themselves up to a light sleep.

Only Hops and Plana stayed close together.

The birds sang, twittered, fluted and rejoiced for a few hours longer, filled the blue morning sky with exultation, talked over their love affairs, their sorrows, joys and differences. Then the midday spread its hot, brooding silence over the forest.

"How beautiful," said Plana, waking at times from her half-sleep.

"Beautiful . . . but hard," Hops answered each time, and each time added the warning, "Lie still."

3

Plana was not always inclined to heed Hops' warning. She had heard those words too often. She no longer gave them much thought and sometimes even felt herself excited by them. Now and again it happened that the moment Hops whispered, "Lie still," she would jump up and begin to race around in circles.

"You're crazy," Hops would grumble.

To which Plana would retort, "Crazy—with joy."

"You'll find out soon enough," Hops would warn her, "but then it will be too late."

Plana would crouch down immediately. "Nothing has happened yet," she said placatingly.

"But something may happen any minute."

"Well, I'm being quiet now," Plana assured him, and lay without stirring on her bed.

But one night they both witnessed an event that made them tremble.

Huge, silent and majestic, the owl went sweeping over the woods, sometimes high above them, skirting the tree-tops, sometimes very close to the ground.

Never before had either of them beheld so marvelous a creature. Still Hops was distrustful; for some unknown reason the apparition seemed weird to him. He did not stir. As quietly as he could, he gave Plana, who was about to spring up, a sharp warning.

Obediently she crouched down again.

But another little rabbit, about twenty hops away from them, wanted to see the wonderful hovering shadow, and moved, barely visibly, ever so softly.

In an instant he was covered by the owl's broad pinions, was buried under the noiseless and seemingly tender plumage. Had it not been for the brief, feeble cry of agony that pierced Hops' and Plana's ears, they would have thought it a caress.

Like sharp knives, the owl's talons penetrated the

rabbit's slender little body. A few blows of its beak, and he was dead in the very act of being lifted, of being borne off through the night air.

"Horrible," Plana whispered. She was trembling with terror.

Hops waited in silence.

Then Plana understood the warning Hops was constantly giving her. She had seen how one expiates his inquisitiveness, his heedlessness. She was grateful to Hops. In her own blood she now heard an anxious voice whispering, "Lie still."

In the morning several of the mothers came to see their little ones.

Hops, too, crouched again beside his mother and told her the story of the owl.

"Yes, yes," she said thoughtfully, "all things threaten us, all creatures hunt us—and yet we hunt no one."

"Where is my father?" Hops asked suddenly. He felt a longing for a protector.

His mother drew back. "What are you thinking of?" she cried, while her spoonlike ears fluttered nervously in the air. Her handsome whiskers quivered excitedly as she went on, "What sort of rash idea is that! Don't dare to dream of so much as crossing his path!"

Hops conquered the shyness which so easily overcame him. "Why not?" he demanded.

"Why, my child," his mother cried, ". . . he'd kill
you!"

Hops was shocked. It took some time before he
could grasp it. ". . . kill me?" he stammered.

"Don't let him set eyes on you," his mother commanded, "at least, not as long as you're so tiny."

"Why does he hate me?" Hops wanted to know.

"Oh, he doesn't hate you," his mother sighed a
little, "but he's so terribly in love with me: I've got
to be with him constantly, constantly . . ."

Hops sat perplexed. He didn't understand a single
word.

His mother began to explain. "You see . . . I want
to be with my little ones . . . as I am now with you
. . . for at present I've only got you. But he doesn't
understand, he can't bear it! If he as much as sees one
of the babies, he becomes furious. In his jealousy, in
his rage he's no longer himself."

"Did he ever . . . ?" Hops stammered.

"Almost . . ." his mother said hastily. "Almost
. . . Will I ever forget the shock it gave me! But I
managed to save the little thing."

Hops sat silent, brooding. This was a serious
matter which he could not quite understand. It was

painful to hear, and at the same time, it was in some strange way beautiful and thrilling.

"Mother," he said at last, "is that the reason I see you so seldom?"

"Don't be angry with your father, Hops," she answered quickly.

He lay crouched as small as possible against the earth, his ears flattened. "No," he said, "I'm not angry with him . . . I can't be angry with him . . . only . . . to think that I have to be afraid of him, too . . . even of him!"

"Not for long, though," his mother comforted him, "not for long. Soon you'll be big enough. Soon the white star will disappear from your forehead. Then you can show yourself to him without fear, and he'll be very nice to you."

"I'll wait," said Hops.

After his mother had gone, he crouched again beside Plana. But he kept silent about the conversation he had had with his mother. Why should he talk about it? Plana was still such a child. And besides, Hops was ashamed of mentioning that his father was so fond of his mother.

That was an adventure certainly! It lifted the lively Hops completely out of the ranks of his playmates. At one and the same time he learned to know himself and life in all its vastness and peril.

For several weeks past they had all been having a glorious time. Now and again, of course, everything had not seemed so serene. From time to time there was a remote hint of danger. But every day they gained in experience, and every day they better understood the danger signals, even if these were not given especially for them.

When a jay screeched or a magpie began to

chatter, they listened. They knew, of course, that the jay and the magpie were their enemies, but they knew, and knew more exactly every day, that by their cries the jay and the magpie betray the approach of stronger enemies.

The squirrel's loud scolding would arouse their attention. They understood the whispering and twittering of the hedge-sparrows and titmice that darted through the branches of the bushes. And they understood how to flee.

They had mastered nothing on earth with quite such skill as the art of vanishing and hiding themselves beyond all chance of discovery.

And nothing on earth was so necessary to them.

The impulse to resist any living creature, to defend themselves, or to fight even the weakest opponent, never stirred their little rabbit hearts.

Their defense consisted of watchfulness; their resistance was the quickly awakened sense of fear that shot through them; and flight, their artful, dodging flight, to which they took in an instant, was their way of fighting.

Then came the adventure that swept Hops along with it.

He was stitting in the narrow open glade around

the salt-lick where he and the others so happily fore-gathered.

A thicket that was almost impenetrable, though not very broad, separated the glade from the meadow.

At that early hour in the morning, nearly all of them were refreshing themselves at the lick.

While the others, Rino and Olva, Murk and Lugea, Trumer, Plana, Klipps and the rest, were crouching on the bare, ocher-colored earth, and lapping the wonderfully refreshing salt, moist with the early dew, Hops sat in the middle of the trough. Buried in the earth, it contained the pure salt-block, held firmly in place by the bright-colored clay.

Hops was sitting right on top of the block, enjoying himself immensely.

At times the others would start a brief game of tag, then settle down again and lap eagerly. A few hopped off into the grass that grew so thick and tasted especially spicy in that particular spot.

But Hops remained sitting in the middle of the trough.

Hops had grown to be a lusty fellow and, whenever an opportunity offered, loved nothing better than boldly and greedily to stuff himself to the full. Often he was so plunged in gluttony that for whole moments he would neglect that prime rule of every rabbit's existence—timid cautiousness.

Suddenly he noticed that all his comrades had scattered.

It flashed through his mind that he had heard the danger signals of the jay and squirrel. Now, though they were silent, he seemed to hear them, and went numb with fear. Above him, in the old beech, a squirrel ran along a stout branch, sat on the extreme tip that swayed gently, held both his fore-paws pleadingly in front of his glossy, white breast and screamed down at him, "Almighty tree-trunk! Are you still there!"

He instantly whisked around again and scampered into the thick foliage high up in the top of the tree, so that all you could see of his bushy tail was a thin red streak, twitching among the leaves.

Hops remained motionless.

His heart began to beat wildly.

He breathed in the wind so deeply that his whiskers twitched violently. Nothing! The wind brought him no scent.

Hops raised his ears.

Then, opposite him in the tall woods, where a light wind was stirring, he heard a very soft crackling in the trampled, tender underbrush, heard a very gentle pattering and rustle of footsteps. Two-legged!

Hops sat up on his hind-legs. He sat up straight as an arrow, his long ears erect, his whiskers, his handsome whiskers, aquiver, his clear, round eyes so wide open in their anxiety that you could see their whites.

Then, between the tree-trunks in the tall woods, he beheld the gigantic, mysterious being who walks erect on two legs, Him whom every creature in the forest fears more than any other.

The monster was already quite close, slinking cautiously, insidiously and with terrible menace, nearer and nearer.

Hops remained rooted to the spot, spellbound with fear.

Even the little rabbits had already learnt that this strange and terrible monster was their lord, as He was the lord over every creature in the forest. They knew that with one terrifying thunderclap He could hurl annihilation from afar. Only recently, when the stag Gobbo had been struck by His thunder out on the meadow, Plana had been sitting close by. Gobbo had leaped into the air above her, so that the red sweat, which spurted from his torn lung, spattered Plana, and her ears and flanks were quite soaked with blood.

In a flash the memory of that incident merged with the feeling of fear that held Hops numbed, his numbness gave way and, with one long bound, he sprang out of the trough, plunged into the grass that swished moist with dew around him, and strove to gain the thicket. When he had reached it, he breathed deeply, grateful for the comforting shelter of the thick plant growth that concealed him.

Again he sat up on his hind-legs, raised his body, with its spoonlike ears, bolt upright and peered at the horrible figure standing among the tall trees on the opposite side of the glade, lying in wait.

Hops felt himself well hidden in his moment of need, but still not entirely safe. The proximity of the weird creature filled him with dread; the fear that made his pulses throb would not let him lie quiet. He whisked about and began to scurry rapidly through the thicket.

His one thought was to get away from there. Far away!

Suddenly there was a rustling beside him. Something made a leap and snapped behind him. Hops heard distinctly the clapping-to of a pair of murderous bony jaws.

An enemy's scent poured about him, poisonous, acrid, stinking, paralyzing.

A fox!

He had been crouching to one side, and among the thick bushes his spring had missed Hops by a hair's breadth.

Instinctively Hops doubled in a loop in the direction of the danger, but past it.

He led the fox to make a full circle. Meanwhile Hops had gained a little headway.

He rushed off.

Out of the dangerous thicket whose tangles might in some way delay or impede him! Out onto the meadow where his path would be clear!

As he emerged on the green expanse he was filled with confidence that he had strength to flee, and with a joy in which fear was strangely and disturbingly mingled.

Hops bounded straight ahead in a perfect series of elastic leaps. He looked handsome as he ran, charming in his youth, in his unqualified determination to escape, in all his motions in which the easy and graceful effort of running was visible.

A pair of hares were sitting on the meadow, two does were standing there.

Hops perceived them only as misty shapes, and it was as misty shapes that everything flitted, dissolving, around him.

On he ran.

The fox was close behind him. Wholly taken up with the prey, which he had thought so safely within his grasp that it could not possibly elude him, he followed Hops.

Now . . . ! now . . . ! he would catch him! Now . . . ! now . . . ! he would know the joy of feeling its warm flesh between his teeth, of snapping the quivering creature's neck while its piteous death shriek rang in his ears like a festive song.

Right before him he saw Hops' round white cotton-tail bob up and down, saw that longed-for bright impudent little knob of a tail dance enticingly ahead—Hops' rabbit banner, flaunted in running. That, above all, the fox would have liked to seize and tear to pieces.

But then Hops circled once more.

It came so suddenly, so surprisingly, that the fox, in full pursuit, blundered some distance to one side.

A short, yapping sound of annoyance escaped him.

He changed his direction and saw the white ball

still bobbing airily up and down through the grass. Only, it was a little farther away now.

Hops had heard the fox's yelp. He heard the grass swish behind him, heard his pursuer again drawing nearer to him. He circled again.

Then he raced away, straight across the meadow, eager to get to the thick wooded strip opposite. Then right through it, in order to reach the broad clearing beyond. Once there he would make a fool of the fox. And if that didn't succeed . . . his thoughts stopped.

He made a fine sight as he scampered over the damp turf, leaving behind, as the grasses bent under his bounds, a trail as thin as his thin little body.

His fore-paws extended parallel and straight. His head appeared to nestle between his feet. His ears lay very flat, pressed close against his body and covering nearly half his back. Only his long hind-legs, that scampered invisible, drove him onwards. His fore-paws hardly seemed to touch the ground.

Everything in this complete little creature now cried: Hurry! Hurry! Hurry! Cried: Flee! Flee! Flee! And cried it with the most complete finality.

Hops grew maturer during that mad race, grew more and more from moment to moment. The impelling fear that governed him grew vaguer the faster he scurried away, and there awoke in him unconsciously the feeling that he was fulfilling his destiny.

He was fleeing for his life.

The thick strip of woodland was successfully passed. Before Hops lay the broad clearing, above which only a few isolated birches, ashes and beeches towered.

Hops ran on. But the blood was beginning to hum in his head and ears. His heart and the veins in his neck were throbbing, deafeningly loud. It was hard to get his breath, and it rasped his mouth and throat, which were slowly beginning to parch with a burning pain, and tore his panting lungs. The muscles in his legs were growing lame, spasmodic.

A longing to throw himself down and sleep crept over him. A guilty feeling took possession of him because he was running away, because he was striving to escape—a feeling of guilt because he was in the world at all.

But fear dominated him again; he was completely overwhelmed by it and it drove him onward.

Presently it was fear alone which still kept him running.

He ran circle after circle. He dropped into thickly-overgrown, deep hollows, lay still for whole moments, started up again, raced in the direction from which he had come, back, and again appeared in some place the fox had not expected.

His white bob-tail darted, a little less lightning-like now, among the low dogwood shrubs.

Suddenly the wind, against which he was running, wafted a horrible scent to his parching nose. It was He, He who walked upright, He the annihilating lord of the forest.

Hops lost all hope. In desperation he doubled back. He did not succeed in running another true circle, only an abbreviated arc that led him back to the fox.

Then the thunder crashed.

Hops crouched down, flattened out with terror and, shrinking together, saw the fox turn a somersault before him.

Then there was silence.

Lying on the ground, his breathless flanks heaving, Hops listened to his own panting. He was ready; he had not a vestige of strength, nor the determination left, to flee. His fur clung clammily to his body, wet with sweat from running, from fear and the trembling anticipation of his end. But the thunder had not struck him, had not even been aimed at him.

The horrible smell of the mysterious and mighty

monster grew sharper, exciting as touch, grew gradually stronger and stronger.

Hops lay still, merely raising his dead-tired face, twisted with pain, while the handsome white whiskers that bearded his upper-lip began a wildly quivering movement. He snuffed in the bitter message of that scent.

But he did not stir. He was at the end of his strength, completely submissive. That restful pause, the slow recovery of his breath, the quieting of his pulse, the slowing down of his heart's throbbing filled him with an ecstasy such as he had never known before. His cramped muscles began to relax. His legs, that had been stiff and painful, grew warm again, seemed filled with a wonderfully pleasant prickling sensation. Hops was no longer master of his exhausted body. He had exerted it to the utmost, driven it beyond its strength. Now his fatigued body held Hops in its power. A pleasant dreamy condition spread through him and baffled his will. A delicious intoxication clouded his senses.

Hops felt the terrible scent drawing nearer and nearer.

He heard the footsteps of the two-legged one. But, as the terrifying monster passed right beside him, Hops lay motionless.

Without astonishment, his mist-clouded eyes watched how He stooped, picked up the still fox by the neck, and carried it off.

Hops sank into a sleep that was somewhat deeper than usual.

5

Meanwhile all sorts of less exciting things had been happening to the others. Even before Hops was aware of the approaching monster, they had whisked, in due time and without panic, under the protecting bushes. They crouched close to the ground and He did not perceive them, they lay so flattened, so silent.

He did not see their eyes round with fear, did not observe the slight, quivering movements of their stiff white whiskers, did not hear the violent throbbings of ten frightened little rabbits' hearts.

All but one of them were on the far side of the

tall trees, through which He had come and among which He remained standing.

Only one found herself near Him.

That was Plana.

Of course it had to be her to whom something unpleasant happened. Of course!

Plana was a pretty little thing. All the rabbit boys liked her, and even the other rabbit maidens treated her kindly. She was such a droll creature, so cheerful and good-natured. She never began a quarrel with anyone, and never even gave occasion for a dispute.

Yet Plana was thoughtless, flighty and absent-minded and at times seemed not to know what she was about.

Of course the others thought Plana a little stupid. But at bottom she was not stupid at all, merely thoughtless.

Thus, when the disturbance began in the glade, when the warning cries of the jays, magpies and titmice left no doubt that He was coming, she did not creep with the others into the thicket on the far side of the salt-lick.

She was sitting close to the open woods. She realized that she had to flee and hide herself and simply ran in among the tall trees where He was slinking.

With the instinct of her kind, she flattened herself

against the ground, she nestled gently among the soft sods as only Plana knew how to nestle.

Then she heard Him, heard his soft footfalls, nearer and nearer.

Plana was aquiver with terror. But she remained motionless.

She merely thought, "Probably I've done something wrong again." Quite downcast she wondered, "Why am I always doing things wrong?"

Then she thought nothing more, could think of nothing more.

For He was right beside her!

The terrifying monster was right beside her, stood and stared and hardly moved.

Nothing but a miserable bunch of lettuce leaves separated Him from Plana, who lay expecting her end.

His scent poured over her like a torrent of water, persistent, bewildering, overwhelming. Plana nearly lost consciousness, overpowered by that strange, menacing smell that at once penetrated the very depth of her being and crippled her.

She saw in front of her two hard, brown monsters. His feet! Those strange, mysterious feet, that were only two and yet supported him, those incomprehensible feet that no rabbit had ever seen before.

Plana went rigid and waited in mortal fear.

She heard His breathing.

He breathed, in fact, very softly. But to her it seemed like a roaring in the air, far, very far above her.

Several minutes passed.

Then Plana attempted something that certainly no one but Plana ever would have attempted, because she did not realize exactly what she was doing.

She bounded up.

Right under his eyes, she bounded up. She simply leaped out into the clearing, leaped, in her bewilderment, right over the trough containing the salt-lick, and rushed towards the thicket.

Everything remained still.

It was not until she reached the concealing shade of the bushes that she sat up, trembling, on her hindlegs, raised her spoonlike ears one after the other, and thought, terrified, "Now what have I done this time?"

He, however, was standing in the open woods, leaning against the trunk of an old oak. He was watching a stag and did not even observe the young rabbit.

But many signals, many ominous signs had warned the stag, so that he decided to stay away from the salt-lick that morning. For a long time He remained standing beside the oak. For a long time not a sound, not a creature stirred in His vicinity. The rabbits lay motionless, flattened against the ground, covered by the thick bushes and the leaves of the blackberry brambles. The pheasants had all run away. The mice took care not to leave their holes in the ground. Only the honey and the bumble bees hummed, the butterflies fluttered through the air, the dragonflies hovered, like wonderful aeroplanes, hung suspended for a moment, darted ahead and hovered gracefully up and down again. In the grass, in the bushes and on the bark of the trees, crept or crawled or marched or hopped the countless, diminutive tribes of ants, beetles, grasshoppers and gadflies. A myriad, fabulous world in itself.

But the jays and the magpies, the squirrels and a pair of crows, the hedge-sparrows and titmice remained aloft at their posts.

Constantly they uttered their warnings. Their outcries, their signals sounded lingeringly through that section of the forest.

Plana lay flat against the ground. Her bewilderment vanished; she became cautious, remained watchful; her charming little nose was constantly in motion, tirelessly examining the air for suspicious odors. Her whiskers stirred gently. Sometimes her ears were lifted, stood bolt upright, like soldiers at a command. Plana was listening. Then her ears would droop again, slowly and limply, like sails that are furled and lowered during a calm.

It was an active kind of repose. There was no other kind for a rabbit.

"I was right after all," Plana thought. "I certainly was cunning. I didn't know how cunning I was." She was quite satisfied with herself.

The watchers, the look-outs and spies, grew silent among the tall woods. For He had withdrawn and the air was pure again.

Again there was some time to browse, to enjoy themselves on the broad, bright field beyond.

With soft peepings the mice were already scampering merrily among the bushes. A couple of moles made their appearance, awkward and surly, but clever and obviously harmless when you spoke to them. One could always talk brilliantly with them. They had agreeable pointed, somewhat ironic faces; and in their thick, dark purplish fur, that was so soft and from which, whenever they came up into the daylight, the particles of earth fell away so cleanly, they looked very distinguished.

Grunz, the hedgehog, sidled clumsily through the

leaves. He was a ludicrous fellow. He wasn't inquisitive, he didn't care to talk to anybody, and he always returned rather coarse but good-natured answers. Of all the creatures who lived in the forest he had the most delicate sense of hearing. It was of an amazing and amusing sensitivity. At the slightest whistle, peep or crackle, he would shrink together as though struck. He was really bowled over. Then he would remain sitting, and his quietly grinning features would take on an expression of profound wisdom.

Pheasants strayed cautiously through the thicket, stopped, raising their little heads to listen, then wandered on.

The rabbits romped out on the meadow again. They would sit quietly for a while at the edge of the forest, lay their ears flat along their backs, and stare up at the tree-tops, stare up at the sky that was slowly beginning to turn green and pale rose.

All of them already had a worried expression, as if they were weighed down with heavy trouble or oppressed by some lingering woe, even while they exulted in the beauty of that morning hour free from danger. Their destiny as rabbits was written in the expressions they unconsciously assumed. In the care-laden attitudes into which they unintentionally fell, during that rare pause, was expressed all the century-old sorrow of the perpetually hunted.

Murk came over to Plana. "You certainly made another fine exhibition of yourself," he said.

"I?" said Plana as if she were astonished.

"You know well enough what I mean," Murk continued. "I wouldn't have given a blade of grass for your chances."

"Don't put on such airs, Murk," interrupted Ivner, coming up.

Mamp and Trumer also hastened over.

"What's the matter here?" exclaimed Mamp, as one born to command.

"Murk's showing how clever he is again," said Ivner. "He's giving Plana some wise advice."

Mamp glanced expectantly and authoritatively from one to the other.

Murk cocked his head. "The girl is so stupid," he began in his clever way, "somebody has to help her."

Trumer had seated himself comfortably. "Why help her?" he said indifferently. "Everyone for himself."

Murk wriggled his ears a little. "I wasn't thinking of running to her assistance, either," he said. "I only wanted . . ."

Ivner interrupted his speech, ". . . You wanted to make yourself out clever . . . you boaster!"

Murk felt insulted. He crept up close to Ivner. "Say that again."

Ivner reared on his hind-legs, his whiskers bristling. "Boaster!" he cried, and immediately began to thump upon Murk's head.

At the first blow, he, too, immediately reared up on his hind-legs and responded with blows on the ear.

Then Mamp set upon both of them. He thumped so fiercely on Murk and Ivner that they rolled over in the grass and tiny flecks of their fur flew about.

Then he turned to Trumer. "And you, what do you want?" he demanded.

Trumer remained tranquilly seated where he was, alternately lifting his ears. "Everyone for himself," he said reflectively, "I'm not mixing into this business."

"Oh, no?" said Mamp threateningly. "Well, here's something for you!" He let loose on Trumer's head and ears a storm of blows under which any other rabbit would have become dizzy.

But Trumer simply bowed his nose to the ground. "Is that so?" he muttered and added indifferently, "Yes, it does seem to concern me now." Thereupon

he stood up so quickly and unexpectedly, and struck Mamp so powerful a blow in the face that he was tumbled over backwards and showed his white belly.

Suddenly all the others ran over. Somewhat astonished, they saw how all four were indiscriminately trouncing one another.

"What's happened?" cried Rino. Klipps and Sitzer did not ask first but plunged forthwith into the fray, while the tide of battle rolled this way and that.

Epi, the smallest rabbit, did not want to take part and ran straight for the bushes.

The maidens gathered around Plana who was sitting, quite perturbed.

"What's the matter?" inquired Nella.

Lugea and Olva were more pressing. "You must know!" they cried. "Tell us right away." They lifted their ears.

"Oh," said Plana shyly, "I'm afraid they're beating one another because of me . . ."

"Is that so?" Nella said sharply. "Is that so?"

At that hostile sound Plana raised one ear, the other drooped, as though broken, along her neck. She kept silent.

A very mild, an almost flattering voice whispered, "Why only because of you, Plana . . . ?" It was Lugea who had crept up softly.

Plana felt uncomfortable and wanted to get away.

"Stay here, dear," Lugea pleaded, "stay and tell us all about it . . ."

The boys had finished their fight and were sitting around on the grass. They were tired out and perplexed.

"It happened . . ." Plana spoke hesitatingly, "it happened when Murk came and reproached me . . ."

Lugea interrupted her gently. "Murk? Was it really Murk? What have you to do with Murk . . . ?"

Plana protested her innocence. "Nothing . . . not a thing . . . only he wanted . . ."

Lugea did not let her go on speaking. Very solicitously, suavely and gently, as if she understood everything, she said, "He only wanted . . . oh, yes . . . he only wanted . . . and he reproached you . . . Naturally, my dear, . . . we know you . . . Silence! Not a word! We know the kind of cunning thing you are . . . and we know how you're lying . . . yes, my dear, . . . you deserve to have someone beat you black and blue for a change . . ."

Nella reared ever so slightly and without any preliminaries immediately began to rain a cruel storm of blows on Plana's lowered head.

The other maidens, too, hastened to mistreat Plana. Their pent-up anger burst forth.

But Plana did not question for a moment whether to let herself be beaten or to resist. She avoided their raging forefeet and simply ran straight into the middle of the meadow. She ran like mad, so that her white cotton-tail bobbed up and down.

It was a surprise.

The others set out after her.

Plana ran circle after circle.

. Mamp, Klipps, Sitzer joined in the race. Ivner followed and Trumer. Rino led them while Trumer decided to bring up the rear.

Plana ran in circles.

The others followed her. Soon there were two, then three circles. And suddenly it had all become happy play again. All their anger evaporated during the race.

From high in the air sounded the hunting-cry of a hawk.

In an instant every rabbit had popped into the thicket.

Trumer was the first to reach the luxuriant green shelter. "Everyone for himself," he thought and chose a bed.

The topmost branches of the trees shone golden, touched by the first rays of the sun.

6

Towards evening Hops returned. He had had a long sleep and did not feel a trace of tiredness. He was in full possession of his strength again.

His state of mind was one he had never experienced before. He felt a stranger to himself as he slowly retraced the way down which he had sped for his life. He recalled each of the terrible moments of his flight. Here he had plunged into a furrow in the earth. He climbed into it leisurely now and found some woodruff-leaves. He nibbled a few of them, reflectively. At the top of the ascent he found some fragrant mint that tasted good. Then he stood for a while before a little spot that at once repelled and attracted him. Several small, frail shoots of hazel, blackberry and silver poplar had been snapped off, others seemed gradually to be recovering and about to raise themselves upright again. Many reddish hairs stuck to the bushes or lay in tufts on the ground, mixed with white cotton. An acrid scent still clung to them and to the earth while near the ground the leaves disclosed some dried red drops, almost pulverized by now.

Hops snuffed. He felt a feverish excitement, yet knew, at the same time, that no danger was threatening.

There the fox had fallen, had tumbled head over heels when the master's thunder struck him.

Hops did not think very deeply about it. It merely passed as a cloud of thought through his mind. The hazy recollection of his somersaulting pursuer, who hung so still, so limp and abject in the air when He lifted him—that hazy recollection and his enemy's last resting-place, before which Hops now sat, merged into one.

Hops felt he had been rescued.

A shudder quivered down his spine.

Hurriedly he left the unpleasant spot.

There were mysteries that made him shiver. He

did not understand them at all. He could only wonder and tremble.

When he had passed through the broad clearing and reached the edge of the woods, he stopped, stood up on his hind-legs, held his ears erect, and peered, snuffed and listened all around. It was a gesture that looked funny; it struck one as comical in its wise old way, but it was really the most serious and discreet precaution.

Then Hops sat erect, his ears flattened along his arched back, sat without any other movement than the vibrating of his whiskers, and remained that way, quite still, for a considerable time. His attitude, his round, smooth head, cocked a little to one side, as if inquiringly, at the sky, his big round eyes full of concern, all expressed Hops' state of mind during one of the calmest hours of his existence. Sitting there, he looked like some timid, worried, humble little shop-keeper whose naïveté and limited experience have accustomed him to suffer much hardship, to endure much mistreatment—while it has never entered his head to defend himself. That miserable insignificant man, who sits on the door-sill of his house in the cool twilight, to draw a breath of air, yet feels the very act of breathing itself a presumption, was the sort of patient creature Hops resembled.

For now he was filled with as much self-confidence as he could ever attain to. What were all the other experiences he had ever been through compared to his adventure of that morning?

He had eluded the one great danger—the greatest that there is—twice, three times. First at the salt-lick —He! Then the fox, whom he tried so long to escape. Then later, a second He. Hops had surmounted the one great danger three times!

Hops experienced an attack of pride. But it was a gentle, deliciously soothing attack that quickly vanished with the twitching of his whiskers.

He knew now that he could trust his swiftness, his ability to run, his cunning in escape.

But at the same time he felt what perpetual watchfulness was enjoined on him.

He belonged to the race of the defenseless, the hunted. But he, Hops, was a sharp lad among this race of the ever-hunted. He had undergone his first serious test that day and meant to become sharper and sharper.

The delicate scent of sappy stems, bourgeoning leaves, of flowers moist with the evening dew, hovered about his nose. Hunger began to stir within him; he disappeared into the bushes. Through the strip of woodland he hurried to the meadow. There he would meet the others. He felt drawn to the meadow, drawn beyond the meadow to the thicket in which he had been born, in which ever since he had enjoyed life, he had made his bed. That day for the first time he had been forced to sleep away from his home in a strange place. Now he was returning again. To the others. To his home. As one who had been saved. As one matured by a great adventure.

He found them on the far side of the meadow near the thicket where they lived. Watching them interrupt their nibbled meal to chase one another playfully in circles, he considered them childish.

Quietly thoughtful, he began to browse, selectly, pleasurably, reflectively.

"There's Hops," cried Plana, surprised.

Little Epi crept up, considered him in amazement and repeated shyly, "It really is Hops!"

Plana and Epi wiggled their ears.

Olva and Rino came up, Ivner and Lugea. Then Klipps and Sitzer.

"Is it you, Hops?" they said to him. "Is it really you, or isn't it?"

Hops considered a stalk of grass, raised himself a little, bit off the fine tip.

The others sat around him. Their ears wiggled.

Hops kept silent.

Then one after the other, Murk, Trumer and Nella came bounding along.

"What's happening?"

"What's the matter?"

Then Nella exclaimed, "Oh . . . Hops! How nice!" She turned to Trumer, "Just think . . . Hops!"

Trumer let one ear droop. "Awfully important!" he said. "A real event!"

Hops turned to him, "Yes, it might well be called an event, my dear fellow."

Suddenly Mamp was standing in their midst. He was not surprised, he greeted no one, he didn't wiggle his ears. He stood challengingly in front of Hops.

"What event are you talking about?" he demanded.

"When the fox was right beside me," Hops answered, bounding up just as challengingly to Mamp.

"The fox?" cried Klipps and Sitzer, Rino and Ivner, terrified.

"Close beside you . . ." screamed the maidens.

A shudder passed over all the rabbits. They crouched and lay flat against the ground.

"Terrible!" sighed little Epi.

Only Mamp and Hops remained standing, confronting one another.

"And then?" demanded Mamp.

"I escaped from him," Hops continued grandly, "and he was . . ."

"Be glad you did," Trumer interrupted in an indifferent tone. "But what good does it do me, what good does it do any of us, that you escaped? Everyone for himself!"

Hops wanted to speak.

"We saw how stupidly you acted . . ." Murk put in gratuitously.

Hops turned to him with a bound. "*I*, stupid?"

"Yes, you were," Murk insisted, "this morning at the salt-lick . . ."

Mamp went him one better. "Don't boast, my poor Hops!" he said. "You were sitting in the middle of the salt-lick, right in the middle of it. Yes, you were . . . you didn't even notice that He was sneaking . . ."

Hops kept silent. He was offended.

Meanwhile Murk ended with conclusive superiority, "No rabbit deserving the name could be as imprudent, as light-headed as that."

Mamp agreed and that was a signal for all the others to agree in chorus.

"Only Plana there," Murk triumphed, "only Plana acted more stupidly than you."

Hops was left alone.

He sat disappointed and sulking. He had not been able to tell them the important news that the fox . . . He let both his ears droop. There was nothing in it for him. He would keep that information to himself.

Suddenly Plana was sitting beside him.

"Oh, Hops," she began, and there was an overtone of coyness in her plaint, "oh, Hops, the others think I'm stupid. Do you think so too?"

"No," Hops replied, feeling the sympathy that one misunderstood creature has for another. "No, I can't believe that of you, Plana."

She crept closer. "Do you know . . . I was only absent-minded . . . and then . . ."

She told him the whole story.

When she had concluded, they heard the thin voice of little Epi saying, "Plana was very clever . . . very clever . . . wasn't she?"

Hops listened intently when Plana spoke of Him.

"No," Hops said at last, "I didn't see Him as near, as dreadfully near, as that, of course, but . . ." And he related all of his big adventure.

Plana listened breathlessly, while Epi uttered sudden diminutive squeaks of admiration and astonishment.

Hops was immensely satisfied with the profound impression he had made.

From then on Plana and he felt closer to one another. And little Epi was their faithful companion.

7

The summer wore on, grew heavy with the heat of the sun, brought days in whose splendor all the scent of the leaves, of the ripening berries and fruits seemed to shrivel up, and nights in which forest, meadow and field, revived beneath the gentle dew, drank back their own cool fragrance.

The rabbits roamed far from the thicket, beyond the clearing, among the crops waiting for the harvest.

There were acres of potatoes. The maize reared its wildly rustling leaves like a cultivated jungle, and the kernels on its cobs were bursting with sweet, milky sap. Its slender stems a golden yellow, the rye stood laden with splendid ears. The dark-green heads of cabbage, bunched like roses, grew close to the earth.

A time of glorious revelry and carefree joy.

The rabbits did not always return to their accustomed beds but lay down in the midst of the teeming abundance, were completely hidden, ate and slept, romped about a little, playfully, ate some more, slept some more.

Many other creatures visited the fields also.

The deer often remained until broad daylight and lay during the day among the high sainfoin. Pheasants came every morning and evening in regular processions, haughty with the metallic sheen of their plumage. On some a white ring adorned their dark glossy necks; but the royal pheasants, with their plumage of flaming gold and black, and their extremely long, sweeping tails, recalled priests in their mitres or princes in full regalia! They loved the maize fields, lay all day long in them, feeding on the juicy kernels. Early in the morning one would hear the splintering bell-note of the cock, and again at evening, when they sought the trees where they roosted.

At times the princes of the forest, the elk, appeared in whole herds. The tips of their crown-like antlers shone white as ivory, while the pearly tines grew darker and darker from the sap of the young ashes, alders and silverpoplars against which they were constantly beaten.

Every creature round about the meadows knew when the elk came. For their smaller cousins, the deer, were always terrified by them, would utter cries of fear and take to flight.

"Baoh . . . ba-oh! Baa! Baa! Ba-oh!" The cries would ring out on all sides, would recede and re-echo from the forest a long while after. Particularly when some nervous old doe could not calm herself at the appearance of her gigantic relatives.

The rabbits knew about these things and were amused by them. With the first loud bleat of terror, "ba-oh," they would merely twitch their ears at one another and say, simply by the play of their whiskers, "The elk are here!"

But they, too, avoided the mighty visitors as much as possible.

The elk were very distinguished and never engaged in conversation with anyone. They came at night under the glitter of the stars, or when the pale moonlight cast its spell. They strode up majestically as if the field were their exclusive property, so that the others could not help having a feeling that they were robbing them. With the first gray morning light they withdrew into the forest again.

The rabbits were very friendly with the lively little partridges. The young ones surprised them by the brotherly way they kept together, by the closeness with which they followed their parents about and the sociable fashion in which the families got along one with another.

Only Trumer expressed disdain for the modest, earth-brown little chicks, speckled with rusty red. "Everyone for himself," he repeated his rule of life.

But little by little even he came to respect them.

They took flight only when pressing danger required it. Then they would rise with a loud rustling of wings and fly, whirring, for some distance, to drop down again in some safer place.

Whenever there was danger, all the rabbits would run, everyone for himself, in the same direction.

Or they would listen, their ears pricked up, as soon as one of the many watches that the partridges kept uttered its short cry of warning.

The tender calls of the cocks, the gentle, loving chatter of the partridge mothers to their young ones, their soft cluckings of content, were pleasant sounds, enlivening the solemnity of the harvest fields, as they lay quiet beneath the fiery blaze of the sun.

What adventures, what experiences, what terrors and perils occurred in the blissful, calm serenity of the fields!

A mole pushed its way up into the light. It appeared blind, yet suddenly, with the most unexpected swiftness, fell upon a thoughtful frog that was sitting, with rapidly pulsating throat, amidst the murmur of the leaves.

The red streak of a weasel in tremendous haste would slither past like a snake and soon after the terrified squeak of some poor little mouse would be heard.

Cautiously prowling, dangerous and bloodthirsty, the cat would slink up. Before anyone could see her, she had clawed a young rabbit. It was difficult to escape her.

Sometimes a stray dog would come eagerly hunting, rummaging through the maize and rye stalks. But the dog did not have the same soundless tread and attack. Reeking almost audibly, it would noisily grope its way in, making an uproar as it sprang after rabbits, partridges and pheasants. It would never stop barking while it ran after its intended prey, so that it set up a wild clamor and everyone had plenty of time to hide.

The fox went to work with more method when he streaked through the fields. He would be very quiet, would sit silent for a long time, waiting for a little mouse. He knew how to scrape the mole out of its shallow dwelling, how to catch the pheasant at the very moment it was taking wing. The fox nearly always claimed his victim.

Yet, in spite of these things, the summer was glorious.

One morning the forest sweltered. The fields steamed as if the night had brought no coolness. The ground, the undergrowth, the trees were parched; the fields dusty-dry. Not a call sounded in any direction. The pheasants were silent as, awakening, they fluttered down from their roosting-places. Their splintering, metallic bell-note was nowhere to be heard, and, for the first time, one could observe that the plaintive sound had a joyousness all its own. So late in August, there were very few birds left singing; that day it was perfectly still. Not a magpie chattered, not a jay uttered its quarrelsome screech. Only at rare intervals the harsh caw of a rook sounded high up in the air or from the tree-tops, and even it was briefer than usual. Not a wood-pecker exulted. Even the twittering of the little hedge-sparrows and post-wrens in the bushes grew feebler and at times ceased altogether.

Deep red, like a round flame, the sun rose, in-dolently, and slowly. Like a veil, woven of tiny sparks, the hot, dust-laden air encircled it.

The sky arched, shimmering with a greenish tinge like the interior of some massive ball of lead above the earth. The fiery tongues of the rising sun licked it up to the zenith. Soon the firmament grew deep-blue, the tongues of fire flickered out, and the daz-zling yellow sun climbed higher and higher, burned and seared the earth more and more scorchingly.

The last voices died out in the forest.

Even the crickets grew silent. The cicadas were still. Only the wasps and bees were to be heard, droning here and there in the underbrush. Beetles crawled under the branches of the trees and bushes. Flies, dragonflies, butterflies kept close to the ground and the swallows and the swifts that followed them flew very low.

Very few creatures went out into the fields that day, and these soon came back. Even the partridges forsook their accustomed grounds. They sought the thicket at the edge of the forest. For a little while longer one could hear the calls of the cock partridges, the responses of the partridge hens, the timid cooing of the young ones, and the warning cries of their outposts among the leaves. Then everything grew still.

There were no marauders slinking about that day.

All creatures were thrilled to the anticipation of something awful.

What was about to happen the young rabbits did not know. They simply felt that something tremendous was going to occur. They trembled. They kept close to their beds. They were serious, full of fearful expectation.

It was the same with all those creatures that were no older than the year which had begun that spring.

Of course those who had already lived several years on earth knew what was coming. But no one dared to ask them and they themselves preferred not to speak.

Hops and Plana lay close together.

"Terrible . . . !" sighed Plana.

"Unbearable . . . !" Hops affirmed.

From close behind them sounded a whispered plaint of concurrence, "Dreadful . . . !" It was little Epi.

"We've got to lie quiet," Hops said, "running won't help."

"Oh," Plana sighed again, "I couldn't even run now . . ."

"Who could run now . . . ?" little Epi barely breathed.

Slowly the blue disappeared from the sky. A livid grayish-white, that looked like curdled milk, spread overhead and made the sun itself turn pale. Yet its rays burned only the more pitilessly.

In the west appeared a deep bluish-black wall of cloud, advancing slowly and ponderously nearer and nearer.

That continued until almost midday.

The dark wall of cloud had not yet reached the sun but was standing still.

Soon afterwards a wispy, light-gray cloud detached itself from the wall, from the bottom of the rack, rolled itself into a ball, spread out again, changed into many shapes as it blew across the whole sky, trailing the dark, threatening wall behind it until it blotted out the sun.

"Is it night already?" asked Epi timidly.

Plana's whiskers quivered. "Now? Perhaps . . ."

The leaves on the trees began to whisper, the thin branches to sway.

A soft breath of wind blew across the earth.

Plana trembled. "Oh, the leaves . . . I can't stand it . . ."

Hops crouched as close to the earth as he was able. "Now it's coming," he said.

The storm struck the forest furiously.

The roaring of the tree-tops, of the bushes sounded as if the forest were bellowing under the lash of the storm.

Plana, who had bowed her head immediately, whispered, "It's the end . . ."

Hops could not hear her.

A raging and roaring was tossing up the whole forest, an invisible but gigantic fury seemed to be rooting it up. The close-packed, slender trees groaned as they struck each other; the old, storm-tossed trunks creaked loudly, one was deafened by the ear-splitting plaints of stout branches that broke in two, the cracking snap of birches and alders. The tops of the aged oaks seemed ready to fly away in the grip of the hurricane.

Wind-driven leaves, thin dry twigs, splinters from the branches that rained down through the air and whirled over the ground wherever they were driven, raised the fears of the frightened rabbits to numbed terror.

A thin streak of light slashed through the darkness. Immediately there followed a short, deafeningly loud clap of thunder.

After a second's pause, a second flash of lightning and the second crash of thunder sounded as terrible as if the whole world had blown up.

Somewhere in the forest, not far from Hops and Plana, the lightning had shattered an old elm.

Between the lightning and the thunder, the rabbits heard the groaning of the stricken tree; after the thunder they heard its dying sigh.

A heavy rain descended in a widespread, gushing downpour. Once before it had rained, and the tree-tops had shed the water so that only a few drops soaked through, one after another, and the earth grew moist slowly. But now this furious downpour instantly beat through to the ground. No tree-top, no roof of leaves was thick enough to withstand its roaring torrent. Ponds and puddles were formed immediately, and wild little brooks rushed in a moment through the furrows, for, thirsty as it was, the earth could not drink up the deluge fast enough.

The lightning flickered a few more times while the instantly succeeding thunder-claps shook the forest.

The rabbits sat almost insensible, dripping wet. Their fur clung to their bodies, making them look quite dark and emaciated. They felt forlorn and alone and believed they were lost beyond all possibility of salvation.

The storm wind held its breath. The lightning grew feebler, as though it were flashing only from a distance. The thunder followed at gradually longer intervals, faint and very far away, rumbling softly.

Only the rain still continued. It rustled, drummed, pattered and made the rabbits generally miserable.

But under the rush of water, the forest stood calm, seeming to refresh itself in the coolness. It began to smell strongly of earth, of reopened, newly reviving earth.

The rabbits remained troubled, each crouching on his own bed.

Suddenly the rain came to an end. The deafening noise was suddenly replaced by stillness. But through the silence could be heard the plopping of single drops that fell from leaf to leaf, a steady dripping, heard everywhere, high in the tree-tops, deep among the bushes, an angry drumming, very trying to the rabbits' nerves. They were all sopping wet and even now, whenever a heavy drop hit one of them, he would tremble as if he were being scourged, or as if the finger of death had touched him.

But presently the smell of the earth and the wet woods grew stronger and more inspiriting. From the foliage, from every leaf, from every plant, a wonderfully strong and strengthening fragrance was exhaled. It was a joyful suspiration, it was the forest's silent, passionately blissful song.

Once more it was radiantly bright; in the west the rays of a mild sun streamed obliquely through the branches, gently but with enlivening warmth.

At the same time, the tap-tap-tap of drops from the trees and bushes continued and prevented the rabbits' hearts from quieting.

From the highest tree-top the blackbird was already rejoicing; the squirrels scampered like mad through the branches, preened themselves, were uncontrollable in their joy. The titmice, hedge-sparrows, finches and bullfinches flitted here and there, with gay twitterings and peepings. The jay screeched, the magpie chattered, the pheasants ran out into the open.

"Are you there?" asked Hops.

"Do you mean me?" whispered Epi. He looked pitiable.

"Where is Plana?" Hops demanded.

"Oh! Hops," Plana said in a low voice, "what a time that was! I couldn't have stood it much longer."

Murk and Nella went by, shivering. Mamp tottered over faint-heartedly. Trumer ventured forth. They all looked wet, bedraggled and forlorn.

"Come," said Hops to Plana, "come, we'll go out into the open."

He did not ask Epi to come, he came of his own accord.

Plana sat up erect. "Out into the field?"

Hops, who had already taken a few steps, halted. "Into the field? If you want to. But I think it would be better at the salt-lick . . . The grass is shorter there, and you can get dry quicker. It's nearer too . . ."

The little glade in which the salt-lick stood lay full in the warm sunlight. There they met Klipps and Lugea, Sitzer and Rino. Also Ivner and Olva.

An old rabbit was there, too—Fosco. A big, important-looking fellow, stout and impressive, a giant compared with the flock of young ones. He was sitting bolt upright near the strip of woodland and seemed to be almost dry.

The streaming sunlight immediately gave confidence to the poor, careworn young ones.

Plana sat down near him.

Hops and Epi took places beside her.

"It was dreadful . . ." Plana began a conversation with him.

Fosco stirred his ears, rolled his eyes, and wiggled his enormous whiskers impressively.

"Not so bad," he said curtly but in a friendly tone.

Plana was astonished. "Not bad . . . ?"

And Hops observed, "I think it was bad enough!"

Fosco blinked down at him disdainfully. He was twice as big as the little rabbit and probably three times as strong. "Ha . . ." he permitted himself to say, "one has to go through such . . ."

"What!" Plana, who was ready to be astonished, demanded eagerly. "Have you ever been through such a thing before . . . ?"

Fosco moved his whiskers. "Many, many times!" It sounded a little boastful.

"Oh!" Plana crept closer to him. She gazed at him in admiration and sighed softly. "Have you really?"

A faint feeling of jealousy awoke in Hops. "What is considered bad by a person like you?" he inquired.

Fosco sat still more erect, became still larger. He also became deeply earnest. "You don't know the snow . . . and the other . . ."

"What is snow?" cried Plana eagerly.

But Hops received this information doubtfully, ". . . and what is the other?"

Fosco did not stir. "Wait a while," he said curtly.

Plana was flattering. "Tell us a little about it—please."

Hops plucked up courage to be impudent. "Tell us about it—if you know."

Fosco kept silent.

A long pause ensued.

Gradually the rabbits grew dry and felt better than they ever had before. Ivner and Klipps had come up. Mamp and Murk joined them. Later Rino, with Sitzer and Nella, crept over. All were sitting around in a circle, gaping at the high and mighty Fosco. Only Trumer kept to one side. Lugea and Olva remained at a distance from fear.

Fosco kept silent for a long time and let them admire him. Then, when more and more of them had gathered around him, he murmured, "It isn't good—when so many sit together . . ."

Mamp turned away immediately. He felt insulted.

Murk followed him and said superiorly, "The pompous old fool!"

Suddenly Fosco lifted his ears, sat up on his hindlegs and his enormous whiskers quivered beside his feverishly working nose.

"Oh," said Plana, trying to quiet him cleverly, "those are only the gentle deer," and she pointed with one ear to the salt-lick. A whole herd had been standing there for some time, moving their ears, scraping the earth with their hoofs, letting the sun dry their ruddy hides.

But Fosco had disappeared before the others were even aware of it.

Presently a mighty elk strode out of the thicket. He stood for a long while, quite still, his antler-crowned head lifted high, snuffing the air in all directions.

Klipps, Sitzer and Ivner, terrified, fled into the thicket.

"I'm not afraid of him," Hops asserted, but he did not sound very determined or convincing.

"You never can tell," whispered Rino and hastened to slip away to safety.

The does had immediately bounded off, head over heels in their haste.

Hops remained; Plana and Epi remained with him.

Slowly and majestically the elk strode to the middle of the clearing, stood motionless again, then shook himself, so that many little drops of water were spattered from his hide and surrounded him for a moment with a glistening rainbow.

Plana crept nearer to Hops. "He never came before in broad daylight," she said tremulously.

Hops quieted her. "He wants to dry himself, too, nothing more."

The elk again took several steps forward, stopped abruptly and made sure.

Suddenly there crashed the sharp clap of thunder that they all knew.

The three young rabbits sprang, terrified, into the woods.

But they saw how the elk had bounded up. All four of his feet pawed the air as if an irresistible force had lifted him and flung him on high. In his beautiful large eyes lay all his final terror, his pain and an anxious longing to escape.

Once among the thick leaves, the three little rabbits turned round again and peered, full of curiosity and horror, out on the clearing. After another desperate bound, the elk again plunged down on the turf. He had no strength left to flee further. He staggered and collapsed in a heap.

They heard the dull moan with which his life expired.

A shudder passed over all three rabbits. They were bewildered and silent.

A new terror assailed them as He appeared in the glade and hurried quickly to where the stag lay. He stooped silently over the fallen body. Something strange flashed and gleamed in His hand. Then He grasped the dead elk's antlers, lifted its neck and plunged the knife into the insensible, bloody, gaping head, which He opened, to take out the antlers. Then He withdrew as softly as He had come.

The air seemed pure once more, all danger had passed.

But the three did not dare to go out on the clearing again. They stayed together, shocked and wondering.

Little Epi was the first to recover his senses. He crept up close to the other two, very close. His ears were quivering violently, his eyes blinked and rolled, his whiskers twitched constantly, and a spasm often passed from his brow down his little back. Obviously he wanted to say something. At last he began, softly, and, as always, shyly, "Perhaps . . . I only mean . . . perhaps He isn't our enemy . . ."

Plana turned to him excitedly. "Do you think so?"

"Before this He only shot the deer . . . This time the elk . . . I only mean . . . we rabbits jumped in front of Him . . . You, Plana, were right beside

Him . . . He didn't do anything to harm you . . . He's never done anything to any of us . . . I only mean . . ."

Plana turned to Hops. "What do you think?" she asked hastily. "Tell me, what do you think about it?"

Hops considered. He let both his ears droop and stared at the ground while his nose twitched and his whiskers quivered. He recalled how He had saved him from the fox. And when Plana kept pressing him and he had to reply, he muttered, "It's quite possible."

Plana sat bolt upright on her hind-legs, joyfully, clapped her fore-paws in the air and exulted. "That would be glorious!"

"But we have to be on guard anyway," Hops added warningly.

8

A few days later fate overtook Epi.

August was not yet past. The three inseparables were lying one afternoon on their beds, never suspecting how soon they were to be parted.

A rustling and crackling among the bushes and branches startled them. No creature in the forest made a commotion like that.

In a flash their ears, struck by the first sound, stood up straight as arrows.

Then the sound of the two-legged footsteps they knew so well grew audible. They were light steps, the steps of more than one person. The rabbits distinguished five pair of feet in five different directions. Lingering, loitering, then again faster steps. These terrible invaders made no pretense at the stealthy approach of which the rabbits always grew so frightened. Of course they were afraid now, too, and, at the same time they felt strangely bewildered.

The snapping of tender, broken branches, the tearing of trampled boughs and leaves sounded nearer, together with the gentle rustle of the unbroken bushes, springing back into place.

A strange, rousing scent assailed the rabbits. They grew still more bewildered, for even this scent was different from that which poured from Him, was less poisonous, less acrid and exciting. It did not whip the blood to a fever as quickly. Nevertheless, the rabbits were alarmed.

They heard clear, shrill voices at whose power they fell into consternation. Their ears twitched and stood up stiffly. They understood nothing, absolutely nothing about voices, were hearing them, moreover, for the first time, and with tremulous awe, for never before had He given utterance to such tones. They knew only the crashing thunder of His annihilation, that overtook them from afar. Then calls resounded and a high, long-drawn-out screeching that never ended.

The rabbits did not know that these were human children searching for berries in the forest, and they did not know that these human children were singing for joy.

Several of the rabbits began to grow excited and to leap to and fro in the thicket—Murk and Rino, Mamp and Klipps, Ivner and the others. The crackling, rustling, tearing and snapping of the bushes, the tramping of the two-legged creatures on all sides, their maddening, manifold scent, and their lingering, over-shrill, incomprehensible voices drove them frantic.

Trumer, in particular, was quite beside himself. He took long leaps, reared up on his hind-legs; his nose was twitching violently and his whiskers were whirling. "If we could only get away!" he whispered senselessly over and over. "If we could only get away!"

Suddenly he flattened his ears, which till then had been raised bolt upright, and gave himself up to desperate flight. They saw the wide arc that his white tail described on the green grass. They heard his panting, "Everyone for himself!"

He must have run right among the invaders, for Hops and Plana, as well as little Epi, saw the strange figures running in the direction where Trumer flitted by. A roaring shout resounded, so loud that it made the hearts of the three inseparables skip a beat.

But no crash of thunder followed, and it grew stiller.

"Now is our chance," Hops said. He was trembling but determined.

Plana bounded to his side. Epi joined them.

Cautiously they slipped through the spurge-laurel, ferns and wood-lettuce. The fear that had gripped Trumer when he muttered, "If we could only get away!" bewildered them all.

Suddenly two of the creatures were standing right in front of them.

Hops and Plana bounded away from one another, running as fast as ever they could. The waving line made by their gay, white cotton-tails flashed over the low bushes.

The two terrifying creatures uttered a terrifying shout. But they remained standing where they were and did not pursue the fleeing rabbits.

Epi had crouched very flat against the ground. He lay so close to the two powerful creatures that their scent almost made him faint. He was completely bewildered, incapable either of decision or motion. He simply hoped frantically for one thing: that he would not be seen.

But a third creature came up, almost stumbled over him and then the dreadful thing happened.

Epi felt himself seized by both ears, felt himself lifted and hung, stiff with terror, in the air.

He did not know that it was a little girl who held him. He did not understand that this little girl was rejoicing over her capture, did not understand that she exclaimed, "Look! A little rabbit!"

Epi dangled, kicking with both hind-legs at once, which made his movements convulsive. When he saw the big, pale face before him and the other two horribly smooth, pale faces, he went stiff and did not stir.

The blood was humming through all his veins, his temples were throbbing, his nerves were in a wild tumult.

"I am lost," was all that he could feel.

He waited for some pain to annihilate him.

Had the three children known what poor Epi was suffering, they might have set him free, out of pity.

Had Epi understood what they were saying, he might have been calmer.

The children exclaimed, "He's lovely!"

[82]

"Isn't he nice?" they cried. And the little girl declared, "I'm going to take him home."

"What a terrible misfortune," Epi thought.

They did not understand one another at all, the little rabbit and the little children. They were from two absolutely alien worlds, and there was no bridge from one to the other.

The little girl put Epi in her red apron.

No sooner did he feel his ears released than he made an attempt to spring out. But she drew the ends of her apron over him and held them tightly together.

Epi sat in a reddish-glowing twilight.

He was desperate and unstrung; never before in the course of his short life had he known such mad fear, such continuous, paralyzing terror.

Once or twice the ends of the apron were lifted again. Epi looked up but instantly ducked his head again, overcome with fear. Five pale, naked faces were bending down to stare at him. They showed their teeth and made him shudder, for he did not even suspect that those five faces wore friendly smiles.

Then five hands reached for him—horribly naked hands. He had just experienced their strength for the first time, and his heart throbbed as though it

would burst. One after the other, with gentle caresses, the hands stroked his ears, his back, his nose. Very gently they touched his whiskers.

Epi nearly died of agony.

Then the reddish-glowing twilight enveloped him again.

A gentle swaying told him that he was moving forward.

Against one flank he felt the warmth of the girl's body who was holding him.

It lasted a long, long while, and the fear that Epi suffered, like a stabbing pain, lasted also. Far into himself he crept. Once or twice he made sudden, wild attempts to spring out. Always the rosy-glowing prison simply closed tighter over him.

Then he gave up. He was totally exhausted. His head ached; his pulse was pounding but he could no longer move a single limb.

Suddenly he breathed a different, unfamiliar air. A strange scent penetrated excitingly to him. He smelt dust, strange creatures, alien things.

Presently the girl stood still. Again her dreadful voice was booming. The ends of the apron were lifted. Five naked, horrible faces were again threateningly near. Epi waited, trembling in dread of the most fearful thing he expected but had never known.

The five hands simply stroked his fur again amidst shouts that Epi did not understand.

It was agony.

Then the apron ends closed again.

The girl was running. Epi was bounced from side to side and up and down. Nausea began to assail him.

Then, suddenly, broad daylight!

Epi felt himself pushed out of the apron. He was sitting on a bare, white wooden board. All around him were noisy, terrifying figures. He—in every size, big, little and very little! One He was like the one they saw in the forest, with dark hair over a pale face. And with only half his head, it seemed —for the man did not have a hat on.

Epi crouched flat on the board that smelt loath-somely.

His nose twitched, there was a buzzing in his temples, his whiskers quivered; all of little Epi quivered as he lay crouching so silent, his head buried between his two fore-paws.

He was sitting on a table on an open verandah. The cottage belonged to the village peddler and had a narrow, uncultivated garden.

"Nice," said the peddler and filled his pipe.

"Lovely," said his wife.

"So darling," cried the little girl enthusiastically.

Her small three-year-old brother cried, "I want him," and clutched at Epi with an energetic little fist.

He did not resist at once though excruciating pains shot through him.

But the girl tugged the clutching fist away, released Epi's fur from its grasp and cried, "Let him alone. He belongs to me."

Epi sat in tortured expectancy.

Again hands were run along his back. The mother stroked him. He Himself touched him. The girl showed her little brother how to fondle a rabbit.

"Like this," she said, "like this . . . he likes that."

At last that martyrdom was over, too.

But Epi had to undergo still another. The man lighted his pipe. When the horror of it seized on Epi, he twitched and tried to sit upright. But a pair of heavy hands immediately held him down. In this position he remained motionless, struggling against the feeling of suffocation that was choking him.

After a while the girl grasped him by the ears and lifted him up abruptly. Epi was again dangling in the air. But he did not kick this time.

They carried him into a room and set him in a box that was filled with straw. The mother had prepared it. Then they placed a few lettuce leaves in front of him.

It was hard for Epi in the room, in the narrow quarters of his box. But he felt tired, too completely dejected to realize exactly how bad it was. He suffered most from the smell. Everything had the sharp, bitter, biting scent that caused him such panic.

Panic! Epi had to remain crouching in his prison, could not, did not dare to move.

Softly he crept nearer to the lettuce leaves. Even they smelt horrible, were covered everywhere with the horror of that scent. But, weak with hunger, Epi began to nibble them anyway.

"Mother," the little girl cried with joy, "he's eating."

Epi shrank back and let the leaf drop.

"Oh, yes," the mother said, "rabbits grow trusting at once."

9

An assemblage was being held on the strip of meadow near the big oak. It had begun quite accidentally, before the dew or the day came, when the squirrel got into a quarrel with the blackbird, and more and more creatures collected: jays, magpies, the oriole, roving pheasants and rabbits that crept up to listen attentively.

It all began when the blackbird, who had just awakened, flew with her twittering cry from a big branch of the oak-tree. The squirrel, his tail twitching, scampered through the branches and sat bolt upright beside the blackbird.

"You lovely creature," he said to her, "how I adore your morning song."

The blackbird kept silent, cocked her shrewd little head this way and that, and pretended that she did not hear.

The squirrel moved closer still. "I'm talking about you . . . why don't you answer me?"

The blackbird twitched her tail in exasperation and prepared to quit her perch.

But the squirrel cried quickly, "Stop. After all, we're friends."

"Friends?" The blackbird spun round in anger. "Friends? That's news to me."

The squirrel sat bolt upright, balancing with his bushy plume, held both his fore-paws innocently before his white breast and asked in astonishment, "You mean to say you don't know that?"

"How should I know it?" the blackbird twittered angrily. "You plundered my nest."

"I?" The squirrel's face was entirely innocent.

"You ate all my little ones," screamed the blackbird. "They were so beautiful, so helpless, and I loved them so . . ."

"Were those your little ones?" In amazement the squirrel whisked completely around and cocked his head on one side, like someone who hears an astonishing piece of news. "So those were your little ones! Well, they certainly were delightful," he said ingenuously and appreciatively, "very delightful! And they tasted delicious!"

Finches, red-breasts, yellow-hammers, and titmice, who had been listening, now joined in. "You robbed us!" they screamed at the squirrel, the magpie and the jay. "You made our lives miserable."

The squirrel sat bolt upright, held his fore-paws pressed against his breast and seemed as much perplexed as worried.

"Did you ever hear anything like it?" he scolded. "All year long I eat acorns and pine-seeds . . . I love everybody so . . ."

"Go along with your pine-seeds!" they chirped furiously at him from all sides.

"But . . . friends," the squirrel was quite beside himself, "only sometimes . . . it's too much . . . !"

"One must live," the magpie chattered unfeelingly.

"Thief!" the hedge-sparrow shrieked. "Thief!" shrieked the titmice, finches and red-breasts.

"You steal our eggs!"

Below in the thicket, where the rabbits were lying, listening, the pheasants craned their necks. "Who breaks our eggs?" they cried. "Who gulps them down? Who scatters the empty shells all about in contempt?"

"I do," shrieked the jay.

The crow cawed high overhead in the tree-top, "So do I."

"Murderers!" cried the pheasants, "murderers!"

"Insolent rabble!" screeched the jay. "What are *you*?"

"We?" The whole chorus of bird voices rose, frenzied. Outchirping each other, twittering, they denied the insulting charge. The blackbird, the yellow-hammer, the pheasants, all of them cried, "We're not murderers! It's a lie! We're not!"

"Is that so?" The jay was raging to begin the attack. "Well, go ask the beetles, the butterflies, the worms." He laughed loudly. "Go ask the snails, you pheasants, you hypocrites!"

The blackbird and the pheasants grew silent, dumbfounded.

Then the woodpecker drummed furiously on the tree-trunk, and furiously he cried, "That's none of your affair!"

"Do you think so?" hissed the jay. "Do you really think so? Am I to take such insults!"

The woodpecker outscreeched him. "You're a

thief! What are you talking about, you good for nothing scoundrel? Are you going to play the beetles' defendant? Or the worms'? Are they our kind? Have they got wings and a noble intelligence like ours? Can they sing, can they rejoice like us?"

"Well, they're alive like us!" shrieked the jay, screamed the magpie, croaked the crow.

"I suppose *you* spare them," mocked the woodpecker, "you're such sympathetic souls! I suppose beetles or worms or snails, dragonflies and butterflies aren't welcome prey to you? And you're casting slurs on us—creatures like you!"

"But you're casting slurs on us," the answer came ringing back, "creatures like you—on us!"

The woodpecker grew furious. "Because you attack your own kind, because you kill your own kin! You pack of murderers, each one worse than the other!"

From the depths of the earth the mole shoved up his rosy snout. "I'd kill my own brother," he said, "if he happened along and I conquered him. I'd eat him up, too. What of it?"

"I don't care to talk to you, you villainous beast," the woodpecker answered.

"Blood," piped the weasel, "blood! Has any of you any idea how delicious it tastes?"

"Delicious, indeed," the shrew-mouse agreed, and

sat elegantly erect. "Whoever is weak must die," she cried in a delicate piping voice.

"Whoever fails to watch out must die," the weasel agreed.

"Whoever gets caught must die," the ferret gloated.

"Whoever is born to feed us must die," purred the fox.

Everyone grew silent and shuddered. Even the crows, the jays, the magpies kept quiet. The squirrel fled several branches higher and sat almost rigid, balancing with his bushy tail.

"And that's how we live," Hops whispered to Plana, "constantly surrounded by danger and death."

"And we never do harm to anyone," Plana replied.

"What good does that do us?" Hops said. "The less you hurt others, the more you get hurt yourself."

But the woodpecker called down to the fox, "You're not threatening me, you old scoundrel, you're not threatening me! I despise you, you and all the others who cling to the earth."

Suddenly a splendid stag was standing in the midst of the assemblage.

He had come so noiselessly, so entirely against the wind, with such ineffable surprise, that not one of all the watchful, constantly listening, ceaselessly snuffing creatures could understand his appearance.

Wonderful, lofty antlers still crowned his head that shimmered silvery on his brow.

"You miserable creatures," he said slowly, "what is the matter with you? Don't you know that there is never any truce in the forest, only constant pursuit, constant flight?"

It was perfectly silent round about.

"We must watch and ward," he said, "each after the fashion of his kind. And each one will make his own fate."

He had disappeared before the others realized it. Nobody could say how or where he had vanished.

Plana sat upright, her ears raised high. "Who was that?" she asked.

Hops sat, his fore-paws in the air, and repeated dazedly, "Who . . . was . . . that?"

Old Fosco raised his head and whispered respectfully, "He? That was Bambi!"

High overhead, on the topmost, swaying branch of the beech, the blackbird began to sing.

10

"Things won't stay the way they are now . . ." Hops was talking softly to himself.

With Plana he had gone quite early from the field into the woods. They were lying close together, closer than the other rabbits, lying on their accustomed beds while the day grew brighter.

"What do you mean?" Plana asked casually and drowsily.

"A change is ahead . . ." Hops replied, "a great change."

Plana grew more awake. "What makes you think so?"

"I feel it," Hops sighed, "I have a feeling . . ."

Plana tried to calm him. "You're always so worried, my dear . . . much too worried . . ."

"We rabbits can never be too worried."

"Nothing at all will happen," Plana asserted, but she immediately began to feel anxious. She saw how upset Hops was, and his concern, like a spark, kindled her own fears.

"Many things will happen," Hops muttered. He held his head bowed, tucked between his fore-feet, and did not stir.

All of them were larger now, Hops and Plana, as well as the other young rabbits, their comrades. Of course, it would still be some time before they were as stately as Hops' mother or the old fellow, Fosco, but they had grown.

"Many things will happen . . ." Hops repeated. "Don't you notice the bitter-sweet taste that everything we eat now has?"

"Yes, that's true." Plana was surprised.

"Every leaf, every blade of grass, every stalk," Hops declared, "everything tastes different. Everything has less sap, everything begins to be a little dry . . . and everything smells earthy."

"Oh," Plana objected, "there's still plenty . . . plenty of fresh things . . ."

Hops blinked. His ears, laid flat along his back, stirred almost imperceptibly.

"Fresh things?" he said. "Thanks." After a while he added, "That kind of fresh things . . . always makes me feel bad when I taste them." After a pause he inquired, "Would you eat the pale blue flowers on the short, weak stems that have appeared all over lately . . . ?"

Plana was silent.

He pressed her, "Would you?"

A shudder ran down Plana's spine. "No," she cried, "I can't stand their smell. Aren't they poisonous?"

"I haven't seen a honey or a bumble bee or a wasp near those things," Hops said almost peevishly. "A great change is ahead . . ."

"Well, ask your mother . . ."

His whiskers quivered. "Mother? It's a long time since she's been here . . . a very long time. I hardly know her anymore. Who knows if she's even still alive?"

"Then ask Fosco," cried Plana.

Hops shrugged. "Fosco? The old folks won't tell anything. They won't tell anything at all. Or they simply give you hints that make you even more nervous."

Presently the others came hurriedly bouncing up
—Murk, Mamp, Ivner, Nella, almost all of them. A
small, transparent gray cloud was traveling close to
the ground in the thicket and spreading a scent that
bit into their noses, that bit so sharply into their eyes
that there were tears in them, and they had to close
the lids. Beyond in the fields the potato stalks, piled
by the peasants, were smouldering.

Within the thicket a gentle whispering was going
on, a delicate pattering that frightened the rabbits
and gave them no peace. The leaves were falling
from the trees silently, detaching themselves from
the branches, spinning slowly down, turning and
circling in the motionless air, then at last, very softly,
very delicately touching the ground. It was as imper-
ceptible as falling asleep. They lay everywhere on
the brown earth, that was becoming more and more
bare and bore more and more of the dead leaves.
Rusty-red, brown, yellow, almost green leaves that
quickly grew as withered as the rest. They rolled
around on their edges; they bent in upon themselves.
They grew warped, then lost their shapes in the
spasm of death.

Many pheasants came running in from the fields,
still showing traces of some fear they had suffered.
Theirs was the astonished haste of furtive creatures,

together with their constant, never-ceasing watchfulness. In running they craned their iridescent necks and rolled their little, expressive, inquisitive eyes. They stopped and ran on again. Only under their elegant, hurrying steps did the dead leaves rustle loudly.

Several stags came bounding in, with long, graceful leaps, checked themselves and turned to stare out over the fields, their heads held high. Their eyes, too, and the play of their ears, told of something troubling their sense of security. Then they turned round again towards the interior of the forest and bounded on until they disappeared.

One stately buck paused longer. He gazed out across the field. Lifting his legs proudly, he strode to a hazel-bush and angrily scraped the ground, so that bits of earth flew up in a spray. With furious blows his antlers struck the poor hazel-bush again and again, tore the leaves from the branches, wounded the trunk until the whitish-yellow interior wood was visible, while he panted, "Never a moment's peace! Never a moment's peace!"

Everyone who was nearby heard him, saw him, and understood his angry outburst. They all admired with what muscular grace his neck bent in the motions of that savage beating, how his head shimmered, crowned with majesty, and the beautiful somberness of his features.

"If he'd only do it again," Hops murmured, "just once more!"

But the buck very shortly relinquished the hazel-bush and vanished in the deep thicket.

Magpies flew from limb to limb, chattering excitedly.

Jays screeched, loudly, mischievously, over and over again.

Alarm!

With heavy wing-beats the crows rose from the fields, veered in the direction of the forest, alighting high among the tree-tops and screaming to one another, "He! He!"

"What's coming now?" whispered Plana.

"You hear them," Hops retorted. "He."

"Ah! He!" Plana crouched down comfortably in a heap. "Then we rabbits need not worry. He never does anything to us . . ."

"How do you know that?" Hops crouched still flatter.

"Well," Plana answered, "didn't little Epi say . . . ?"

"Epi . . . ?" Hops wiggled his whiskers violently. "Epi . . . ?"

But Plana insisted, "Little Epi was very clever . . . very clever . . . he watched and . . ."

Hops interrupted her. "Where is Epi?"

Plana grew silent, frightened.

There was quiet for a while. Only the chattering of the magpies, the screeching of the jays, the slowly receding cawing of the crows continued and made the silence more pronounced and tense.

With a rushing leap a squirrel dashed down through the big branches of the beech. In the midst of his mad career his shrill voice rang out by fits and starts.

Yet before he had reached the lowest branch, the thunder that they all knew crashed five or six times, one peal after the other, on the fields outside. But it was a weaker, fainter thunder. It crashed thinly, unsteadily, scatteringly.

Hops looked out. His heart grew heavy within him.

Some distance away across the fields He was striding along. Seven of Him, at short intervals from one another, so that His line reached across the narrow side of the field. Before Him two hounds were running back and forth, were standing with one leg lifted, rigid, head and neck pointed up straight.

From the tip of their tails to their muzzles was one straight line.

Then He came nearer, in a row. The dogs sprang free. The line of partridges whirred up. Immediately after, the thunder cracked, and three, four dark bodies fell heavily from among the flying flocks of partridges.

"There, you see," Hops turned to Plana. "He's murdering our little friends. He won't spare us either."

"No," Plana contradicted, "He won't hurt us." She held firm to this hope. "He won't hurt us. Think how He saved you from the fox!"

Hops kept silent, troubled.

"And you know," Plana went on feverishly, "you know, that very day I was sitting close to Him . . . right near . . . then I passed right beside Him . . . passed right next to Him . . . not even fast, for I was paralyzed with fear. Well, did He do anything to me?" She was triumphant.

On whirring wings the partridges soared again outside. Five or six times the low, thin thunder crackled again. Three partridges dropped to the ground. The two rabbits watched the ghastly drama somewhat closer at hand. They saw how the bodies that had been hit twitched and then lay motion-less. They saw how one stricken hen beat her shat-tered wings in agony, struggling to rise, frantic with terror.

A hound leaped on her and seized the little flutter-ing body in its jaws. It did not stir again.

"I tell you . . ." Hops began with a shudder.

But Plana wanted to dull completely the fear that was beginning to awaken in her. "Don't tell me anything," she cried, "I believe what Epi . . ."

Hops interrupted her. "Epi! Stop it! Didn't He capture Epi?"

Plana bowed her head. "That's true . . . true," she repeated, almost weeping.

Hops muttered, "He was the first of us to go . . ."

"Right . . ." Plana whimpered, ". . . right!"

At that moment the loud, whirring flight of the partridges reached the thicket. The sharp thunder came rolling in seven, eight times, one peal after another, from the fields. "If we could only have got in here at once," their gentle voices twittered. "The only thing now is to go on," others urged. Still others complained, "We can't go on . . . we're tired."

A hen-partridge fell to earth from among the hunted flock—right beside Hops and Plana. Both were shocked by the way the little thing struck the ground, so suddenly and so hard; by the way it slowly rose and sat up weakly.

"Is that you?" Plana asked, terrified.

The partridge did not answer, but held its short neck bent backwards. Its tiny head was tilted upwards and its slender bill hung open in pain.

"Are you hit?" asked Hops, terror-stricken.

The response was infinitely gentle, "I . . . don't . . . know." It was a dying voice.

Hops and Plana gazed fascinated at the little partridge that was sitting, struggling before them. Its eyes had grown larger than usual from fear, from anxious expectancy. Its head remained in its rigid position, without moving. Only its opened bill seemed to want to scream forth the torture that was rending its little body, or to cry for help.

Plana couldn't stand it any longer. "Can I get something for you?" she whispered across to the partridge, though she did not know exactly what she could get.

But the partridge's consciousness was already far removed from intercourse with other living things. Its consciousness had buried itself deep in its wounded breast, or very far away. Somewhere. The eyes of the partridge no longer spoke of expectation or fear:

they spoke another, a strange, sad language. It was their farewell to this world. The convulsive attitude of its tiny head relaxed. It drooped slowly, very slowly, with an infinitely wistful, infinitely eloquent gesture, and sank down, gently slipping, limp on its breast. That is how the partridge died.

Outside on the fields, He was drawing nearer in a row.

"Shall we get away?" Plana's whole body was trembling and her ears were fluttering restlessly up and down.

Hops, too, was in a tumult, but he remained motionless. "No," he answered firmly, "He won't enter the thicket. Lie quiet! See if you can keep your ears still."

Plana waited stolidly in her hollow.

A rabbit sprang up outside and ran along in front of His line into the woods. He ran circle after circle.

The thunder crashed. The rabbit kept running. Twice, three times it crashed again. The rabbit kept running. The thunder pealed a fourth time. The rabbit gave a start but kept on running.

Breathless, he ran into the bushes, ran as far as Hops and Plana, and they saw that his flank and his white belly were all red and clotted with blood and dust.

"Rino," screamed Hops.

"Rino," screamed Plana at the same moment.

"I must go on," Rino panted. But at that instant he fell, as if struck by lightning, and kicked a few times, as though he imagined, lying there on the ground, that he was still running. Then he lay still —a small, brownish-white streak on the dark brown earth of the forest.

"What's the matter with him?" asked Plana timidly.

Hops kept silent.

He sat up on his hind-legs and raised his ears erect. His features were troubled and his eyes had a careworn expression. "Now's the time for us," he said.

Plana was sitting up like her companion.

Suddenly she whispered, "Look, over there! Over there! Isn't that Trumer?"

Hops glanced out and let his ears drop. "Yes, it certainly is."

"Strange that he should have remained out there so long," Plana said in surprise, "he of all persons!"

Meanwhile Trumer was running in at terrific speed, while the soil of the field rose in a dust behind him, in the frenzy of his flight. Cunningly he ran big and little circles. "Everyone for himself!

Everyone for himself!" was the thought that bore him forward as though on wings.

One short, sharp crash of thunder sounded, only one.

Trumer turned a somersault, then another, for the momentum of running carried his dead body along with it.

He lay stretched out in a furrow on the field, the white wool on his belly turned up to the sky.

Hops and Plana hurried away. Deep into the forest.

They were already far off when the hounds came rummaging through the thicket to fetch Rino and the little partridge.

11

A time came when the sun rose late and set early in the evening—a sun that seldom shone at all. All day long the sky would be covered with thick, gray clouds. Rain poured down in torrents so persistently that there was not a dry spot in the whole forest.

The rabbits sheltered themselves under the washed-out roots of trees, crept into narrow holes and were nowhere visible.

Then violent storms roared again through the forest, tearing, lashing, rending and snapping trees and branches together. The rabbits were still more terrified by this tumult. But the storm-wind dried the ground, dried the trees. Drops no longer fell from the branches and the rabbits were not compelled to live in constant nervous terror.

But the nights grew colder and colder. In the mornings a white shimmer lay over the short, yellow meadow grass that grew more and more withered.

The leaves on the tree-tops and the bushes turned yellow, brown, rusty-red. The great change that Hops had forecast began to take place. The pattering down of falling leaves was a steady whisper through the lovely days, through the still nights in the forest.

Nowhere was there any quiet now.

Even when the ground was only partially dry, Hops and Plana would roam out onto the meadow at the edge of the forest, where the bare, broad stretches of the earth ran, grass-covered and straight, into the distance. Those stretches bore many suspicious tracks, and many an arousing scent, left only recently, clung to them. Sometimes, too, He came that way as Hops and Plana were sitting among the tansy. But it was not dangerous, for they could hear Him from far off. There on the broad fields He moved without the cunning stealth that they had come to associate with Him, and which made Him so terrifying. For this was obviously His world. Hops and Plana began to love those broad stretches, in

spite of His tracks and in spite of His scent. They
would go there in the evening and remain all night.
In that way they were spared the weird whisper of
the falling leaves. Here there was nothing but the
fields on which now and again they searched for
forgotten potatoes. If morning surprised them, they
had to watch carefully because of the hawk, but
they soon reached the sheltering forest. Moreover,
the crows and magpies, which they no longer needed
to fear, gave them signals of warning. Even at night
they could see the owl from afar and could hide
themselves.

There was less danger in the fields.

One night Hops and Plana were sitting in the
middle of a broad stretch of land.

The starry sky arched its mighty vault over the
fields, and the black, rigid wall of the forest stood
near at hand and silent.

Hops and Plana had just satisfied their hunger.

They were not nibbling anymore, for the abundance had vanished and there was nothing more to
nibble.

They already had some difficulty in finding tasty
food. Whenever they did find something now, they
would settle down and eat sensibly until they were
satisfied.

"It's so beautifully quiet," said Plana.

Hops let both his ears droop and said, "It's generally quiet here."

"You can breathe for once," Plana went on, "and feel yourself safe."

Hops grew thoughtful, held his head tilted abruptly upwards, twitched his nose and said, "We can breathe all right. Oh, yes . . . but we rabbits can never feel safe . . . never! Don't ever forget that!"

Plana crept up very close to him. "You're so clever," she said, flatteringly, "much cleverer than I . . ."

His whiskers quivering, he answered, "I simply want to live . . . and I want you to live, too, Plana."

Away off in the distance two fiery points gleamed, close to the ground. Shortly afterwards they grew to big flaming eyes. A moment later they were two palely glowing suns. A bright radiance streamed dazzlingly from them, along the surface of the field.

Hops and Plana barely had time to lift their ears, to sit up on their hind-legs.

The two suns raced on, the dazzling glow grew more blinding, drawing nearer.

A hollow rolling, creaking and whirring swelled deafeningly.

Both rabbits ran, stumbling, half mad with fear, amazement and curiosity.

They were bathed in the white, alluring light of those two suns that fascinated them, and yet filled them with terror.

It was not until the last moment that Hops, almost blinded, bounded to one side into the hollow that served them as a trail.

Plana leaped after him.

The monster thundered by, rattling amidst its stench. A moment and it was gone. A moment and the dazzling light of its two suns, gleaming from afar, was already dancing and glancing at a distance across the fields.

Soon it had disappeared entirely.

Hops and Plana lay in the darkness that now seemed to them much darker than before.

"What was it?" Plana asked in bewilderment.

Hops, too, was struggling for composure, "A . . . terrible . . . danger!"

But Plana insisted, "What was it?"

With an effort Hops collected himself, "It was . . . He!"

Plana did not believe him. "He? . . . No, that can't have been He."

"It was certainly He," Hops persisted, "what else could it have been?"

Plana grew heated, "I can't tell you that! But He . . . ? He? . . . It never can have been He!"

Unaccustomed to contradiction by the gentle Plana, Hops, too, wavered. "If it wasn't He . . ." he began.

"It wasn't," Plana interrupted.

"Then . . . then I don't know what it was," said Hops.

"We ought to be thankful that we escaped," Plana said impressively.

Hops wanted to guard his superiority and concluded, "You see now how right I was. Our kind can never feel safe."

12

One night the forest resounded with strange noises. They were deep, full sounds, and quite short. They sounded here and there from the most tangled thickets, they rose from the middle of the clearings.

The young rabbits were startled. They had never heard anything like this before. But they were hardly frightened at all. They knew that the voices belonged to the forest, that there was nothing threatening in them. They understood. The voices were calling, "Come." They were calling, "Where are you?" They were calling, "Desire!"

Hops and Plana soon discovered to whom they belonged.

The whole forest cracked and crackled under the trampling of the restless elk.

The rustle of withered leaves revealed their comings and goings.

The slender branches of the bushes snapped when one of the elk kings barred the way.

The antlers of the bounding beasts hammered against the stems of the bushes that made a clear, lively, ringing sound.

The elk princesses wandered by, young and old. Their manner was quite innocent, apparently indifferent, as if they were aware of nothing at all, as if they were merely driven by an unappeasable hunger. But they were just like the elk, astir every hour of the day and night. They were always pretending to be seeking nourishment. They plucked the leaves from the bushes, remained for long intervals beside the young trees, affecting, with outstretched necks and noses lifted high, to reach the lower branches, then nibbling at them so that the boughs, which had been tugged down for several moments, flew back with an audible snap. Or they would lie down in the open woods and remain there till a stag startled them. Or they would bound in senseless flight, in wild commotion, through the forest, through the midst of the thicket, and out across the meadow. It left everybody in fear and excitement; like them, everyone took madly to flight. Then they saw that it had all been nothing more than a coquettish sally, a whimsy.

But one night, in the hour before day and the dew came, loud cries boomed through the distance. They began with deep, short outbursts, three or four, one after the other. A low moan from the chest, that seemed to burst, then the cry rolled out, dark, powerful, tremulous with its own strength, seething with passion.

Other elk answered here and there in the distance. The same deep voices. Then lighter, fainter voices that soon grew mute.

Hops and Plana sat very close together near the edge of a little glade. They saw Brabo, the majestic, pacing from the thicket to the glade, from the glade to the thicket. On his proud, branching antlers, shimmered sixteen bright ivory-hued prongs that rose smooth and perfectly bare from the branches, which were almost black and thickly covered with big black pearls. His thick-set neck was hidden beneath his shaggy mane. He held it outstretched, held

his head outstretched, so that his mighty crown of
antlers lay almost on his back. And while he bellowed, roaring, moaning, his great, soft, beautiful
eyes flashed wildly. The blood flooded his head and
colored the whites of his eyes red. The breath puffed
in a cloud from his steaming mouth, so that the
thunder of his voice hovered visibly about his head.
And all his marvelously graceful body, radiating
energy, steamed in the chill of the morning with
the fire of his passion.

Brabo had five princesses around him. They stood
trembling, enraptured, in tense anticipation.

The season of love had come.

Meanwhile, through the tangled undergrowth,
Zebo was slinking, cautious, timid, but nevertheless
obstinate, urged on by desire. He was slenderer than
the gigantic Brabo. He had no stately mane, and his
antlers had only eight white prongs.

He was young.

He slunk up to the very edge of the glade. Very
close. In the middle were standing the five princesses, and Brabo was jealously guarding all five of
them.

Zebo advanced as noiseless as a cat, as furtive, as
stealthy and watchful as a fox. Presently he was

standing, screened by the trellis of thinly-leaved, tall bushes, peering out.

Yonder—ah yes, yonder was the lovely Astalba—there with the others. But the others didn't concern him. Let Brabo keep them. Only she, the splendid, the desired! Only she . . . !

Astalba seemed to expect Zebo.

As if by chance, she detached herself from the herd and strolled past the thicket.

Brabo had just turned his back. His cries were booming in the other direction.

"Come," whispered Zebo, "come, beloved! I'm waiting, come!"

Astalba glided up to him.

Hops and Plana heard them talking, in pressing haste and excitement.

"Let us flee," pleaded Zebo.

"I don't trust myself," Astalba said hesitantly.

"Only a few steps, softly . . . then, as fast as we can," he implored her.

She remained undecided. "We won't succeed . . ."

"Don't you love me?" Zebo begged.

"Can you ask?" Astalba answered quickly.

"Then come, come with me!"

"I'm afraid . . ." She broke off in the middle of her words.

For Brabo had turned around meanwhile, had missed the charming little princess immediately and was roaring horribly, "Where is Astalba?"

He was beside himself, but he knew that there was not a moment to lose. His bellow boomed out incessantly. "Where is she? Where?" He raged around the four remaining females. He beat them with the flat of his antlers. They huddled together fearfully.

Then he saw Astalba reappear, innocent, guileless, as if she had just made a little excursion to while away the time.

But he knew what that meant! Oh how well he knew women and their wiles! He bellowed, furious with anger, and hurled himself into the thicket. "Who's there?" he kept roaring incessantly, his voice choking with fury. "Who dares to come here? Who's there?"

In his heart of hearts was a tiny hope that there would be no one and that Astalba's faithfulness might be confirmed. But at the first bound into the bushes he snuffed Zebo's scent. And immediately after he heard his rival who was attempting quietly to withdraw. A furious bellow broke from Brabo. The bushes cracked, rustled and snapped under the fury of his onrush.

Then right before him he perceived his opponent's glossy flank.

Opponent? Was he really an opponent? That mere nothing! That weakling! He was a thief! A common thief!

But Zebo had no sooner heard the storm that came raging behind him than he gave up his soft slinking and vanished with a crackling and snapping, bounding in flight, swift as the wind.

Brabo checked himself.

Let him run! The important thing now was not to leave the women alone! Back! He turned and hurried, panting, to the narrow glade.

"Let him come back, the sneaking thief!" he thought. "I'll get him sooner or later . . ."

Exultant, with the feeling of a conqueror, he strode up to the princesses. His cry resounded triumphant and vibrant with passionate tenderness.

Hops turned to Plana, "Let's get away from here!"

Plana's ears rose quickly. "What for?"

"One can't tell what may happen," Hops said. His ears hung down limply at both sides of his neck. His charming whiskers were twitching nervously. Hops looked excited.

But Plana was in high spirits. "What can happen?"

she asked loftily and sat bolt upright, her ears raised high.

Hops blinked at her and thought her bewitching. In matters affecting little Plana, he had become almost will-less of late and had begun to notice it. It gave him pleasure to submit to his friend. Only in things involving caution did he still strive to assert his will.

"They are so powerful," he began after a short pause, "they are so powerful—these kings—and they are absolutely frantic. It's dangerous . . ."

"No, it isn't." Plana was happy and quieted him. "They don't pay the slightest attention to us."

Hops flattened his ears thoughtfully. "It might happen . . . without their meaning to . . ."

"No, no," cried Plana, "let's stay . . . just a little longer. I'm so curious . . ."

"If only it isn't too late then," Hops warned. For the first time he decided not to go alone and immediately. For the first time he did not compel his friend to follow him simply by beginning to run. He was surprised at himself.

"How can it be too late?" Plana retorted, "we're watching sharply. Besides, we're small and so quick . . . and you're so . . ."

A booming cry ended her speech in the middle. It came from behind them. It was another king, not Brabo. The newcomer was standing, to all appearances, not very far away. Scarcely a few bounds.

The two rabbits crouched flat against the ground.

Once more the cry rang out, boomed out on four, five, frightful, roaring, opening tones—dreadful, like the announcement of some mighty decision.

Brabo tossed his antlered head high. He stiffened to iron. All five princesses stretched out their necks, alarmed and faithless. Then Brabo answered the challenge. His voice was as powerful as that of his invisible foe. "Come on!" he roared.

"Keep quiet, and get along with you!" was the thunderous retort.

Brabo was furious. "I'm standing here, waiting for you."

"Don't wait," roared the other, "save your life while you can."

Brabo stamped several times impatiently, a series of short, angry stamps. Then the cry rattled from his breast, "Save yourself, you coward!"

"Boaster! Idle boaster!" came the raging answer from quite near.

Brabo knew this encounter would decide things. He had fought many such battles and had always triumphed. Hence his lordship year after year. Hence he possessed the right to choose his own mates year after year. No one in the forest had ever yet been able to deprive him of that right. Not one out of all those who were forever striving to. He stood still and listened to the other's snorting breath, heard the snapping of the branches, the rustling and crackling of the dry leaves under the hoofs of his oncoming foe, heard the sharp, clear sound with which the other's antlers struck against the branches and tree-trunks.

At last he plunged out, furiously at first, dashing out headlong. Then, at the sight of his opponent, slow and threatening.

Brabo recognized him at once. It was Pasto, with whom he had fought two or three years before, and who had fled so precipitately with a gash in his neck. Through Pasto's thick mane Brabo saw the long, livid streak of that old wound. He noticed that Pasto's antlers were very lofty, if not so wide-spreading as his own. And he noticed that his crown bore ten long, gleaming, white prongs.

Of course, at that moment, both stags were deaf and blind to all else. Had He been there then, He could very easily have stretched them both out on the green turf. For it was against one another that both were now tensely concentrated. Their fury had reached a point at which it almost resembled serenity, at which it was keen-sighted, full of the most exquisite consciousness, the most exquisite deliberation.

Pasto attacked, meaning to drive his antlers into his enemy's flank, but his lowered forehead struck hard against Brabo's lowered forehead. There was a hollow, cracking sound. Then both stood for a few moments, head pressed to head, apparently motionless. But a tremor ran, barely perceptible, over their bodies while each concentrated every ounce of strength in his neck.

Tense, with the utmost intentness, the princesses watched the two antagonists and shifted nervously from one leg to another without actually taking a step.

Spellbound, Hops and Plana watched the wild drama. They never once noticed that Zebo had again slunk up quietly and was hiding at the edge of the bushes. They did not notice how Astalba suddenly tossed her head high and listened and then, very slowly, with pretended innocence, drew nearer and nearer to the thicket.

Brabo and Pasto broke away from each other at the same moment, made a simultaneous lunge at each other's flanks, and, by a simultaneous parry, collided once more forehead to forehead. But more violently, more furiously than before.

"Now!" whispered Zebo through the net of leaves. "Now or never!" It sounded louder than before, more excited, fuller of hope. No one heard it but Astalba. She stood hesitating.

"Come," he urged, "come quickly, and we're free!"

Astalba moved her legs, undecided, but driven by desire.

"Quickly, beloved one!" pleaded Zebo. "We'll be lucky."

Astalba cast a quick glance at the two combatants, assumed an expression in which falseness and joy were mingled, and disappeared in the thicket.

There was a slight rustling, scarcely audible. But Brabo heard it, for all his senses were incredibly alert. "She's running away from me," he thought. A wave of jealousy surged through his blood. "She wants to get away! She wants to be untrue!" His seething anger scalded him cruelly. "I'll get her back," he raged. "I'll get her back soon enough! But first I'll settle accounts with this scoundrel here! First I'll beat him to a pulp!"

Recoil! Attack! Recoil! Attack! Brabo had lost his control and patience. Time and again he sought his

enemy's flank, his chest, his shoulder, strove to grapple him, to rend his belly, and time and again he encountered only Pasto's rocklike forehead. Time and again they clashed their antlers together with a dry, clear sound. Once there was a peculiar snapping noise. Something white flashed before Brabo's eyes; a tremor passed over him and a shudder of despondency. Under Pasto's mighty onset a prong had splintered from his crown. But he had no time to reflect, and no longer the strength of spirit.

He heard a loud rustling and crackling that grew distant. He knew it was Astalba, who was lost to him, who was running away with her young lover. But what did Astalba mean to him now? Only little remnants of jealousy, of pain, of his outraged right of possession provoked him in the fury of the fight. He was fighting for the mastery he had so long maintained. He was struggling for his proud existence, for his own majesty, without which he could no longer live. He was struggling for love. Of course not for love of any one maiden, whether her name was Astalba or anything else. It involved love above all, but it involved everything!

Again they were standing forehead to forehead. Pushing, pressing, their heads lowered farther and farther. Their breath came in loud snorts. Their eyes stood out immense, bloodshot and flashing fire.

Brabo felt that he was obliged to give ground to maintain his balance. He felt that he was giving way. Had to give way! Compelled by the other's strength, which was superior to his own. Unspeakable astonishment spread through him, an insidious mortification awoke in him and threatened to weaken him. Desperately he resolved to try a sudden charge, a mighty onslaught. It couldn't be possible that he was beaten. Impossible that the other should compel him to give up his place, him, Brabo!

But before he even knew what had happened or how it happened, Pasto charged into his side. While Brabo was staring vacantly into space, fog before his eyes and his brain reeling, a mighty thrust tore a gaping rent in his mane, a second blow ripped open his shoulder. He sank to his knees. He felt the red sweat running hot down his leg.

Then frenzied fear, such as he had never known, gripped him. Everything vanished in the torrent of his fear—pride, love of power, everything. If he could only get away! Only save himself! It bore him up, helped him to recover, allowed him to avoid Pasto's fresh, murderous attack. It made him capable of fleeing, despite the sharp pain that burned in his neck and shoulder. In his wild haste he leaped towards the nearby thicket, as majestically, and with as much male grace as if he were unhurt, safe and sound. But it was best not to look at his face which was distorted with terror, or his eyes that were filled with grief. A few steps and he heard his pursuer behind him. Then he heard the thunderous roar of triumph of him who from now on would be lord.

Brabo was lord no longer.

Humbled, ashamed, humiliated, he tottered through the undergrowth. Where it closed most impenetrably above him, Brabo sank heavily to the ground. The fever from his wounds mounted and shook him. More painful than the fever, the sense of his own powerlessness shook him. Like a bitter dream, the memory of his season of glory swept over his soul—how he had been the foremost, the most powerful in the whole range of forest; how he had chosen his princesses and had made them queens; how everyone who had contested his lordship had been forced to flee or been laid low; how everyone drew back in awe before him. Past! Even the place he had just filled as lord of all, even his princely predilection for the contrary little Astalba now seemed to him remote and past.

He was old. A half hour ago he had not known it. He could not quite grasp it yet. Nevertheless there could be no doubt of it: he was old. He would no longer love the world, or the love that had spurred him on, and yet had cast him down. He would abide alone.

When Hops and Plana had crept very softly past Brabo's couch, Plana halted a moment to ask, "Did you notice that his eyes were full of tears?"

Hops hurried on. "No!" he said quickly and ran.

He did not want to talk about it; he was too much upset.

13

At the window of the room in which Epi was pining in captivity hung a little bird-cage. In the cage was a linnet that had been caught outside in the forest.

Epi lay quietly on the bare board bottom of his narrow box, a couple of cabbage leaves always in front of him.

The linnet sprang restlessly to and fro in its narrow prison. From perch to perch. There were only two. But the linnet hopped from one to the other all day long.

The people of the house were delighted and said, "How lively he is!"

But the linnet was by no means lively. He was desperate and half-mad with longing for freedom, with yearning for his kind.

What had happened, how he had come to be there he did not know, he did not care to know. But the mortal terror that had paralyzed him when the dreadful hand clutched, closed round, and released him only in that tight, transparent prison, still shot quivering through his body.

At first he fluttered wildly against the cord bars, hurt himself, ruffled his plumage against them and broke several feathers. Little by little he grew tired, feebler. Finally his fluttering ceased, but he could not quiet himself. Early in the morning, on waking, he dreamed of his free life, and in the evening, too, when he put his head behind his wing to sleep. Those wings were no longer of any use to him. They no longer bore him up as once they had. When he recalled how he used to dart through the air in the fragrance of the flowers, in the warmth of the sun, in the coolness of the shadows, he thought he would die of sorrow. Then, in the torturing confines of his prison, began that tormented and endless hopping from one perch to the other. Between times now and then, there would be a brief fluttering—but very seldom and only when some mistake made him think his prison-gate was open. For hope never left the linnet's breast: some day there would be a hole in the prison, some day a way out would appear. Constantly, confidently the little bird waited. The hope kept him alive. But when his homesickness for the forest threatened to strangle him, he began to sing.

Before the linnet became his companion by the window, Epi had lived a sad and lonely existence. He had become quite dull and gloomy. All day long and all night long Epi dozed; his rapid movements ceased.

During the early days, amid the terrors that surrounded him, he kept thinking constantly of Hops and Plana. What the two of them were probably doing, how things were going with them out there in the forest.

He spent many hours considering over and over again the error he had committed and through which he had got into this horrible situation.

"I shouldn't have waited so long," he thought, "but Hops and Plana stayed on their beds, too . . ." No, he rejected that. "Hops and Plana were up and away at the right moment." He brooded over it. "I should have been up and away, too. Hops was always preaching that . . . for us rabbits it must always

be up and away! Next time they won't catch me . . .
not me! Next time . . ." There he faltered.

Presently he was lost in dreams again. How he
would bound away! Out into the fields! He would
find his way to the forest! He would surely find his
way! He would run towards the smell of the forest.
Sometimes the wind, that breath of the forest, blew
into the room. Sometimes something like the smell
of the forest earth, a message from the thickets, was
wafted through the window. Then Epi would raise
his ears quickly, his whiskers would quiver feverishly, his eyes would roll around in his head. He
would bound out of his box, frisk about the room,
become almost daring as he tried the limberness of
his legs—until they caught him and put him back
into his box once more.

How he loathed those bare boards, soaked through
with uncleanness. How he hated the cabbage leaves,
the pieces of potato, the turnips they flung him for
food. Everything was contaminated by His touch,
stank of Him, for whom Epi felt such oppressive
fear, such deep aversion. He ate always with a choking disgust.

A wasp blundered about the room. Epi listened
with rapture to the whirring of its wings.

"Do you come from the forest?" he asked.

"Forest?" hummed the wasp, "I don't know . . . maybe . . ."

"Oh no," Epi murmured wistfully, "oh no! If you were from the forest, you'd know it."

Another time a beetle hummed in.

Epi started up.

"Are you from the forest?"

"From the what?" answered the beetle. "The forest? From the dungheap!"

"Miserable creature!" thought Epi, and paid no further attention to him.

Again a butterfly fluttered over the sleeping Epi. He heard the delicate whish of its wings, awoke and cried, "I greet you . . . you are from the forest, aren't you?"

"Yes," answered the butterfly and capered in the air. "Yes, I do come from there."

"Oh!" Epi was so moved that he could not speak.

"What do you know about the forest?" said the butterfly.

"I? I?" Epi stammered. "I beg you," he was completely unstrung. "I beg you, settle down for a moment."

The butterfly alighted, opening and shutting his wings. "But only for a moment," he said.

"Please wait," Epi was pleading, "I must tell you . . . I want to ask you . . ."

"Impossible." The butterfly rose. "I can't stand it here!" He capered high into the air again. "How did I ever come to get in here?" he called down to Epi.

"Only listen to how *I* came to get here . . ." Epi called beseechingly to him.

"That's none of my concern," answered the butterfly. He fluttered gaily to the open window.

"Are you flying back to the forest?"

But the butterfly no longer heard him. He was already outside, in freedom.

Epi sank back into his despondency. At times it seemed to him as if the whole world, Hops and Plana, the other rabbits, all that had not actually been real, but merely a dream of his longing—and one that was darkening. Epi let it darken. He no longer possessed will enough nor sufficient desire for life to cling to what had been.

But when the captive linnet in its narrow cage was set upon the window-sill, Epi once more awakened from his torpor. He raised his ears bolt upright, he snuffed inquisitively in the direction of the little bird. He sat up on his hind-legs, and his whiskers, which had become yellowish, brittle, insensitive, twitched more violently than ever. For the linnet came from the forest. Epi smelt the gentle odor given off by the tiny bird's plumage, that unforgettable breath of freedom, of the tree-tops, of the uncontaminated branches, the never-profaned leaves. It was very, very faint, that smell. It grew fainter with every hour and finally vanished altogether. But Epi had breathed it in passionately. That freshness, that glorious message from his home pierced Epi to a heart that was bursting and throbbing with the memory of it.

At first the linnet would not be talked to. He beat like mad against his bars and heard nothing. And his wild desperation drove Epi back into even more desperate sorrow. He sat silent, gnawing inward at himself, kept his poor, sorrowful eyes fastened on the linnet, that was fluttering to pieces against its cage, while Epi's whole being raged and raved with the little imprisoned bird. Epi seemed very quiet when one looked at him. But his small, unhappy soul was lashed by a storm of longing, of impatience, of the bitterest complaint and chafing. In those few hours Epi declined more than he had in weeks.

The linnet gave up its senseless fluttering and began its ceaseless hopping to and fro.

Epi called up to him, "Do you come from the forest?"

Again and again he asked. No answer. Epi did not lose patience. He sat erect on his hind-legs as long as he was able, which was not very long. He raised his ears and let them fall again. He snuffed with his nose, twitching violently to catch the last vestiges of that beloved smell of home. And he did not cease to repeat his question, "Do you come from the forest?"

At last the linnet peeped, "How does that concern you?"

Tenderness shone in Epi's eyes as he replied gently, "I, too, am from the forest."

"How does that concern me?" The words sounded morose and angry.

Epi was completely crushed. For a long time he sat bowed and silent. Presently he sighed, "The forest is beautiful."

Then the linnet began to sing.

Epi listened. He felt agitated to the point of bursting, he felt tranquilized to the point of bliss, he was glowing through and through with rapture, and yet felt cruelly depressed.

Later there were conversations between the gentle Epi and the contrary linnet.

"Do you know Plana and Hops?" Epi inquired. The linnet replied curtly, "No."

"Are you sure?" Epi persisted gently, "Just think for a . . ."

The little creature repeated abruptly, "No."

Epi was astonished. "How can that be possible? You come from the forest and don't know Hops . . . don't know Plana . . . ?"

"Who are they?" the linnet permitted himself to ask.

"They are relatives of mine," said Epi with pride, "my good friends."

"Do they look like you?" the linnet demanded.

"Oh!" Epi cried, deeply moved. "Oh! They are much handsomer, they are truly beautiful."

The linnet sprang to and fro. "It may be so . . . it may be so. We, we who fly, we pay very little attention to what crawls on the ground."

Epi felt ashamed. All that day he brooded in silence. But the next morning he said, as though he were giving an answer to something he had just heard, ". . . and yet even you were captured . . . just like everyone else . . ."

Again the linnet began to sing and again Epi was plunged into that strange intoxicated mood in which all the vitality of his life seemed to ebb away.

They often talked with one another, the two captives, more fully and amiably. The linnet began to

have an understanding of the earthbound creature
that could not fly or sing, of its simplicity, of its
sorrows and its joys. Epi learned to know the life
of the winged songster that could see from on high
and knew the raptures of unbounded space.

But this very rapture, that in the anguish of his
heart he could just divine, made him more and
more incapable of enduring his fate.

"You'll bear it longer than I . . ." he said.

"Why?" peeped the linnet.

"Because . . . because . . ." Epi stuttered, "because
you . . . your song is enough to . . . free . . . your
heart . . ."

Even then he spoke with difficulty. All day long
he sat there, never taking a bite of food, trembling
in every limb. Once the little girl who had captured
him bent over and noticed that his food remained
untouched and that he was shivering. She lifted
him up gently, held him in her arms, stroked the
poor rabbit, who merely trembled more violently,
and said to him, "What's the matter with you?"

She called her mother. She came, stroked Epi and
said, "What's the matter with you?"

For a while they both fondled him, and both kept
repeating over and over, "Well, well, what's wrong
with you?"

The everlasting question that human beings ask dumb animals, quite tenderly and altogether without understanding. The everlasting question which never takes into account the mistreatment suffered, doesn't want to, and is satisfied, in some mysterious way, that it remains unanswered.

Toward evening Epi lay exhausted in his box.

The linnet was singing.

In his song the forest took form, with all its wild enchantment; passionate yearning for freedom was in his song, burning desire for the tree-tops, for the sun, for the cool, green shadows.

In his bitter-sweet trance Epi lay spellbound. He began to see his beloved thicket, he thought he was beside Hops and Plana. Many rabbits came running up together to greet him. On the meadow of his childhood the games of tag began anew.

Epi raised his ears erect, he bounded more wildly than any of the others.

Actually he merely gave a feeble twitch.

While the linnet sang, Epi rolled over quietly on his side, stretched out and did not ever stir again.

14

A few days later Hops and Plana were wandering in a distant part of the forest far from their haunts.

All the rabbits were now roving, for there was less and less food, and the expectation that it might be elsewhere drove them on.

They met Ivner, Murk and Nella.

Murk had grown big and fat. He looked like an old man. He had lost all his impudence and superciliousness. He was morbidly nervous. He suffered from insomnia and acted with such meekness, was so tremulously and timidly attentive, that all the rabbits who came near him were shocked and embarrassed.

"Friend Hops," he said, "friend Hops, forgive me . . ."

"What shall I forgive you for?" inquired Hops in amazement.

Murk's voice was fairly gasping with a sentimental zeal for reconciliation. "Well, once I insulted you."

"Me?" Hops was still more astonished. "Me? I don't remember anything about it."

"Yes," Murk insisted, "of course it was a long time ago. In the old days . . . when we were still young . . ."

"But we *are* still young," Hops consoled him.

"Ah, no," Murk interrupted him, "I am young no longer . . . not I." He shuddered violently in every limb. "Do you recall, friend Hops, how you returned to us? You had something to tell us, something about your adventures with a fox. It was then that I insulted you."

"Oh!" Hops parried, "I forgot that long ago."

"You are so good," Murk whined. He turned to Plana. "And you are so beautiful," he flattered, "you're wonderfully beautiful." He burst into contrition. "And to think I insulted you, too! Yes, yes, to be sure. It was on the same day. I remember distinctly."

Plana's whiskers twitched gaily. "I never think of it anymore!" she wiggled her ears. "Don't think about it either, Murk."

"Ah, now that I see you again, I remember," he said, "and it torments me. Everything torments me . . . everything!"

Plana crept nearer to him. "You had better remember how beautiful it was," she exclaimed.

Murk sighed deeply, "Beautiful! They *were* beautiful times! Glorious times!" He sighed again. "Gone! Gone forever!"

"Nothing is gone!" Plana raised her ears erect. "Be happy, Murk! You're so big and strong!"

Murk disregarded that. "Are you two always together?"

"Yes," Plana said simply, "that hasn't changed either."

"No one," Murk confessed forlornly, "no one stays with me . . . and I can't endure anybody."

He hied himself off at once without farewell, taking lifeless leaps that made a good deal of noise.

Plana stared after him and shook her head. "Such a monster of a fellow," she said, "so strong . . . and so spineless."

Hops sat brooding and replied, "The scar . . . did you notice the big scar on his back? I wonder what can have made it."

Ivner, whom they met soon afterwards, had Nella with him. He had grown to be a lean, sinewy fellow, full of incisive energy, and with humorous leanings.

"My dear little cousin," he said to Hops, "the main thing is not to become embittered—you have to flee just the same."

When Hops suggested that rabbits have it harder than most, Ivner was very much astonished. "In what way?" he cried, his ears erect. "I can't see it." He spoke in disjointed sentences because of his excessive energy. "Nonsense! Everyone has to flee at times. Caution is important for everyone! Just recall your fox! And don't talk rubbish! I wouldn't care to be anything but just what I am!"

Hops felt himself pleasantly emboldened. "Remarkable!" he muttered.

"Why remarkable?" Ivner rattled on. "Don't be stupid, Hops. You always were a little stupid!"

"Pardon . . ."

"Oh, well, let's forget it," Ivner interrupted, "it's all in good sport, anyhow. The main thing is to be frank, isn't it? Melancholy and feeblemindedness are too widespread among us rabbits, take it from me. Have you seen Murk? Yes? Well, there's a first-class idiot!"

"Poor fellow," said Hops, condoningly.

"Well, that was a bit thick," Ivner corrected himself. "But after all, what can really happen to any of us?"

"Plenty," said Hops with conviction.

"Nothing at all," Ivner decided simply. "If you're clever . . . nothing at all! You can get to be seven or eight years old, and no one will do a thing to you."

"Well," Hops felt inspirited by what he heard but remained thoughtful, "well, but most of us . . ."

"Because they're stupid," Ivner interrupted quickly. "At least it's true of the others. Few of them ever reach their natural age. But look at Fosco! Alert! Alive! Cheerful! And he's in his seventh year! A shrewd old fellow!"

They were silent for a while. Suddenly Ivner began, "Just think of it—*our* conscience is clear! We belong to those noble creatures who have a clear conscience. We've never harmed a living creature. Only the deer and the elk are like us . . ."

Hops was skeptical. "What good does that do us?"

Ivner drew his head into his neck, so that his

spoonlike ears lay flat. "The lovableness of inno-cence," he said proudly, "the power of swift flight, the unconquerable defense of cunning . . ."

Hops reflected. After a pause, he asked timidly, "And . . . He?"

Ivner blinked contemptuously. "Oh, He's highly important, I'm sure! What does He have to do with us? He simply plays no role at all."

Hops objected. "No, no," he said, "that's going a little too far for me. That's altogether too irre-sponsible!"

"Irresponsible!" retorted Ivner quickly. "Who's talking about irresponsibility? One can't afford to be irresponsible for a single second. Just mark my word!"

His head lowered and laid on his fore-paws, Hops muttered, "That's just what I've been saying."

"Well then?" Ivner went on. "Well then? Day and night, at every hour, there's constant danger in the forest! But you know that! There's a threat in every bush, in the open fields. There's danger always and everywhere. Yet we go on living! What do you want of Him? When does He ever come into the forest? He? Nonsense! He doesn't belong to the forest. You can hear His step no matter how softly he sneaks. He's so clumsy. Then there's His scent. We can avoid Him. He comes so seldom and acts so clumsily that He's the least danger of all."

"In spite of that," Hops was eager for reassurance, "in spite of that, everybody fears Him . . ."

"Sufficient!" Ivner took him up short. "It's sufficient to fear Him, then you're protected from Him."

He sat upright, his fore-paws dangling, listening with his ears erect, examining the air with his nervously twitching nose and vibrating whiskers, then sat down again in his former position. He looked dashing, like an impudent tough.

"Plana's got to be charming," he said suddenly and gazed over at her as she sat in conversation with Nella. "A delightful creature."

Hops nodded distrustfully. "I'm not giving her away," he said. It sounded ominous.

Ivner continued to stare at Plana. "She's really quite uncommonly pretty."

"She's with me, and she's going to stay with me, understand?" Hops was irritated and ready to do battle.

Without paying any attention to him, Ivner said, "She must be very soft, and very tender . . ."

"That's none of your concern!" Hops shouted testily.

"No," Ivner readily conceded, "no, it really isn't any of my concern. You're right, my dear Hops. I'm with Nella, and Nella is incomparable . . . I wouldn't wish for anyone else."

Placated, Hops glanced at Nella. She was hideous, had unkempt fur, a sloppy appearance and vulgar manners, while quarrelsomeness and ill-temper were written all too visibly on her stupid face.

Presently she hopped over with a heavy, shuffling gait. "Come, Ivner," she commanded, "we're going now. We've been here long enough," she added discourteously.

Ivner obeyed her without a murmur. But he wanted to take leave in a friendly way. "It's nice to have had a chance to talk out our minds to each other."

Nella was already off. Crying, "Leave off your yarning and come along!"

Ivner bounded after her instantly.

"I can't understand what he sees in her," Hops said to Plana.

Plana smiled. "Yes, she has him completely in her power. She's not the least bit attractive and doesn't even pretend to be intelligent. But she rules him just as she pleases."

"Strange," mused Hops, astonished, "such a clever,

such a clear head, such really superior intelligence, and yet he's in the clutches of that slattern. Strange."

"All such things are strange, my dearest," Plana assured him. "No third person can ever know or tell anything about them."

There were a number of pools and ponds in the preserve where they now found themselves, so that the ground was damp, and the grasses in the meadow, the leaves on the bushes were still fresh and full of sap.

One day they met Zebo and Astalba. The two of them were living in the deepest thicket, enjoying a serene and peaceful happiness.

Zebo was joyful and could not conceal a certain pride. He burdened Astalba with his tenderness. He never left her side. He caressed her face and eyes with his tongue for hours on end. He guarded her sleep and rejoiced when she awoke.

Astalba looked more graceful and matronly. She was tender, devoted, poised, and accepted Zebo's love with a constant smile of blissful happiness.

Both made so charming an appearance that Hops and Plana lingered near them.

Since his conversation with Ivner, Hops had become more confident and freer than ever.

One day they witnessed some unusual things.

Suddenly Brabo stood before them, deep in the undergrowth. The wounds in his neck and shoulder and in his right flank had scarcely healed. He looked aged and emaciated.

He appeared to have caught sight of Astalba and Zebo as they lay side by side on their bed. He stretched out his neck and longingly gazed at Astalba, whom he had once so passionately loved, and whom he loved still. A tremor passed over his sick and weakened body as he stood struggling with his impulse to charge and do battle for his loved one. His slender legs quivered with desire, yearning and jealousy. But the feeling that he had been beaten, which had humiliated and broken his spirit, held him back. Very softly he slunk away.

He came again the next day, at the same hour, when Zebo and Astalba were resting. He came the same way for several days, and stood hidden in the thicket, his head stretched forward longingly, his fixed, adoring glance fastened on Astalba. Then he slunk off without making the faintest sound, shyly, secretly, with a gesture that seemed to say he despised Astalba and had never really wanted her anyway. But Hops and Plana saw the sorrow in his still handsome features, read the grief in his great, dark eyes.

15

The leaves had all fallen from the trees. The branches were bare and stretched their naked twigs, as if in desperation, to the sky. The grass on the meadow was a sickly yellow hue and tasted vile. Even the pale meadow-saffrons had shed their flowers.

Only, in the middle of the meadow, a plane-tree spread its branches which were still covered with leaves. To be sure, its leaves were of many colors, from faded green to copper-red, but they still hung from their stems, and the plane-tree was very proud of looking so splendid.

In the morning, thick mists steamed up through

the forest; the paths were gray with them. The sky seemed to be hung with heavy, wet, gray draperies, and the rays of sunlight that did manage to pierce through were very few, lasted but a short while and gave no warmth. Even the sunlight was pale and weakly.

All the birds now sought the luxuriant plane-tree. Magpies gathered there with a subdued chatter. Hidden in its branches, the titmice whispered. The blackbirds, who no longer sang, uttered their twittering cry as they came flying to the plane-tree.

Hops and Plana scoured the meadow for food. They found little and grew thoughtful. Hops' mother was with them. Fosco, too, came often, and the two old folks talked of the hard times that were ahead.

Hops and Plana did not understand them.

"Harder still?" asked Plana, incredulous.

"I should think this was plenty hard enough," Hops said.

"Oh, this is nothing yet," Fosco informed him.

Hops took him for a boaster and kept silent.

But, as if she had read his thoughts, his mother said, "No, really—things are still bearable, but later . . . you can't imagine what it's like."

A flock of birds came flying through the misty-gray, smoky air. They were big birds with long, outstretched necks. The rabbits could hear their voices from far off, long before they were visible. Then, as they flew past not far above the meadow, they saw the wonderful order of their flight. Against the cloudy sky it was like a triangle without a base, like a pair of calipers, whose legs are about half open. Their leader was at the apex, and close behind him followed their long, oblique lines, neck after neck, wing behind wing, breast behind breast.

At the sound of their cries, at the sight of their orderly flight, Hops and Plana raised their ears erect, sat up on their hind-legs, and asked, "Who are they?"

"They are strangers," Hops' mother said.

"They are the freest of all free creatures," Fosco added.

Meanwhile the honking of the wild geese re-echoed, thrilling, ravishing. A wild exultation shrilled through their cries, a deep unruliness, a triumphal pride, a never-sated wanderlust and passionate yearning for all distant lands.

They passed above the bare forest, showering their clamor and adventure-lust upon the creatures who cling to the earth. Long afterwards they could still be heard.

The rabbits listened, silent, enraptured.

"The fortunate creatures!" Hops said with a sigh.

Fosco sighed, too. "Now the frost will come."

Hops' mother agreed. "Whenever those strangers fly out, they bring the hard times with them."

But Mamp capered and kicked up his legs. "What do we care about hard times?" he said.

Mamp was a happy-go-lucky fellow, the liveliest of all the rabbits in the forest. No danger succeeded in dampening his cheerful spirits. He would escape from some terrible adventure, that might have cost him his life, with as much impudent gaiety as if it had been a joke. He was still playing as tirelessly as in the springtime. Companionable though he was, he remained ever single.

He had just nudged Hops' flank with his nose and was racing in a circle over the meadow. "Come on, try to catch me," he teased. He was like a child.

Hops sat quietly; the old folks did not stir.

Again he bounced up to Hops, nudged him, leaped over Plana and challenged, "Catch me! Run, you lazy-bones! That will warm you up!" He raced so wildly that he tumbled several times head over heels. It made no difference to him whether he stood on his head or displayed his white belly as he rolled in a ball. He was nimbler and fleeter than most of the other rabbits.

No one was so alert, so clever, so cautious or so full of wiles as he when it came to fleeing or hiding himself, yet he didn't put on airs, and hardly seemed to take it seriously.

Hops rebuffed him with, "Hard times are coming . . . frost!"

Mamp did not take that seriously either. "Frost?" he said. "What's frost? I've never seen it."

"You'll feel it though," snapped Fosco.

"Have you ever felt it?" Mamp came back at him.

"Plenty of times, unfortunately!" Hops' mother and Fosco answered together.

"Is that so?" Mamp bounded high into the air. "And you're still alive anyhow. Why should I be afraid?"

Plana chimed in. "I tremble whenever I think of the hard times."

Mamp came racing by. "Come Plana, run. Nice Plana, why are you trembling so soon? Wait till the hard times get here."

"It's hard enough already," said Plana, embarrassed.

"What's so hard?" Mamp mocked. "There's not much to eat. Well! Later on there may be still less. That's healthy, though. We won't starve to death!"

He left all the rabbits sitting close to the trunk of the plane-tree among the low bushes, and raced to the middle of the meadow.

A hawk which happened to be flying by hovered for a moment in the air, then dropped down. It dropped like a shot, its sharp talons clutching at Mamp. But they only caught the dry grass. For Mamp had seen the hawk, had guessed the exact spot where it would strike the earth. He eluded it with marvelous skill. Now he was racing off. He ran like mad, but with what presence of mind! He seemed simply to be playing with the huge bird that pursued him close to the ground. The hawk's wings whirred. As it flew so close to the earth, the hawk could get no impetus, but its talons kept clutching for the rabbit, who was always right beneath it and yet bounded away again and again. Mamp ran circle after circle; the hawk had to twist and turn and grew more and more furious. Blackbirds, magpies and jays came fluttering up and flew about, screaming.

Then Mamp bounded into the thicket, in where the tight lattice-work of the bushes hampered and impeded the hawk. Both disappeared. All that could be heard was the angry scolding of the fluttering blackbirds, magpies and jays.

"He's lost!" said Hops.

"Poor fellow," whispered his mother.

Fosco kept silent.

"Nothing will happen to him," cried Plana.

Then the bird of prey mounted high above the thicket, its talons empty. The blackbirds, magpies and crows still screamed around it for a while, as if they were frightening it away. The hawk soared in a wide circle, almost without beating its wings, higher and higher, till it vanished among the clouds.

On the edge of the bushes Mamp's head appeared, his merry face poked out, his spoonlike ears wiggling gaily.

"Nothing ever happens to him," Plana rejoiced.

The next morning there were no leaves left on the plane-tree. They lay in a thick circle on the ground, beneath it. They lay like a cast-off garment, strewn thickly around the trunk: the tree was bare. The plane-tree had not managed to retain one tiny little leaf. It seemed to be ashamed of its sudden nakedness, and to be cold.

The meadow looked as if it were dusted with sugar. This time the hoar-frost did not disappear as usual with the advancing day. On the contrary, white stars and flakes began to dance slowly down through the cold, motionless air. So many of them, that it was difficult to see more than a few steps ahead.

The young birds, who had been fledglings when the rabbits came into the world, were unfamiliar with this white fall of ice-cold stars. They were blinded by the flakes that settled on their eyes; they felt caught, as in an icy grip, by those that fell on their backs and wings.

They soared up like arrows, trying to escape them. When they had convinced themselves how futile such efforts were, they strove to reach a branch, and huddled there silent and frightened.

The young rabbits, too, had never been through such an experience, and were astonished. For a while they crouched without moving, rapt in contemplation. Then they observed that the whiteness, lying on the ground, piled up higher and higher all about them. They observed that their heads and backs were covered with it, and that a biting cold pierced them sharply from this whiteness.

They grew uneasy and tried to run. But they felt how difficult it was for them to move through that cold, white mass.

"What is it?" asked Hops, alarmed.

"It's the hard times," his mother answered.

16

At first it was perfectly still. Hardly a sound was to be heard. Only, at night the owl's hoot sounded. It seemed like a lament. Actually, however, the owls were calling tender greetings to one another. Then there was the bloodcurdling cry of the screech-owl that pierced every nerve. But the screech-owl meant no harm by it; frightening others was simply his little joke.

A few mild days came. The south wind went roaring through the forest and swept the clouds from the sky, so that it was all blue again and the sun shone. Under the sun's rays the snow melted very quickly and the wind soon dried the ground.

It was glorious.

"Are these your hard times?" laughed Mamp, more impudent than ever.

"Just wait," Fosco warned.

"I'm waiting," Mamp teased, "I sit around all day and wait for your terrors."

"Have you had enough to eat?" asked Hops' mother.

"Isn't wood almost enough?" Mamp wiggled his ears good-naturedly. "I find it stays longer in the stomach . . ."

"Look at the elk kings," cried Hops, "even they are starving."

The elk and their princesses stood in the tall forest, nibbling the bark from the ash-trees.

Mamp stared at them intently. "Starving?" he said. "I should say they're feasting."

But the peace was shattered, for He came into the forest.

He approached noisily in a band. Titmice, magpies and crows had given warning signals in advance.

"Let's move farther on," Mamp said as the first thunder crashed rather far off.

The news spread fast: He had aimed at pheasants this time, but He was not averse to rabbits, either.

A herd of terrified elk charged into the thicket, halted and snuffed the air. They grew more and more nervous the nearer the thunder pealed.

"They won't stop here," said Mamp, "let's run with them. Watch out!"

"Why do you want to risk it?" Hops objected. "He's everywhere out there."

Mamp crept along the edge of the thicket, then came back and reported. He had found out that there were only a few game-beaters, placed in such a way that the pheasants could not run out.

Sitting up as tall as he could, his ears elegantly erect, he delivered himself of this speech: "Let us all make our getaway, pheasants! I mean it for your own good! Let us get away! As for me, I'll run between the legs of the tall gentry, then I'll be quite safe." He spoke pompously.

The elk charged in wild flight. Without hesitating, Mamp hurled himself into their midst and rushed away with them.

There was a trampling, a crackling, a snapping of dry branches. Then the cries that He uttered. Then silence. No thunder.

Mamp had saved himself.

Those who remained behind were thrilled and breathless.

"As if he'd done the same thing who knows how many times before!" said Fosco after a while.

"A clever boy, that Mamp," Hops' mother declared.

The thunder kept crashing nearer.

"I believe we can risk it now," suggested Hops, who had long been uneasy and troubled.

"We have to," cried Fosco, his fears mounting.

All four rabbits ran.

Outside in the forest lane they heard the roaring of the game-beaters. But the rabbits simply separated farther, one from another, and ran on. A few pheasants ran after them.

They reached the next thicket where it was still and solitary. They did not stop but ran through the second, through the third; and passed at an easy run through the fourth and fifth thickets.

The thunder rumbled steadily, fainter and farther away.

The rabbits did not remain in one place, they went farther and farther on. High above them flew those pheasants that had escaped without being hit.

At last they arrived at a great assemblage. Elk were standing close together, haughty and exclusive, as if they were alone in the world. Deer were keeping timidly to one side. Several pheasants were strutting back and forth excitedly, with apparent aimlessness. A fox slunk slyly through the confusion and vanished before he could spread terror.

Mamp was sitting with a number of other rabbits, as lively as ever.

"Well," he called out to them, "wasn't I right?"

Whole salvoes of thunder pealed in the distance.

"Do you think so?" said Hops' mother vehemently. "Our brothers are dying now."

"But we're still alive," Mamp answered quickly. Then he grew embarrassed. "Do you remember," he asked Hops, "how Trumer always used to say: 'Everyone for himself'?"

"Trumer is dead," Hops declared gloomily.

Mamp felt that the conversation had taken too serious a turn. He nudged the tired Hops in the side. "Look, one meets old acquaintances here."

Lugea and Klipps were approaching. A little farther off Olva lay flat on the ground. On the farther side Sitzer was crouching all alone.

"Oh! how nice!" cried Plana, delighted. "What a strange meeting!"

Meanwhile the thunder crashed faintly.

"Oh! Plana," gushed Lugea, "how pretty you've grown, and how handsome Hops is. Do you still live out there on the meadow? Yes. Well, we've moved

in here. Klipps and I, that is. It was my decision.
Though after all, it really was his, wasn't it, Klipps?
Oh! he lords it so . . . you have no idea!"

No one else could get in a word.

Klipps made an attempt which, as usual, failed.
"W—we are de—de—delighted. . . ." He could get
no further. He stammered, but whether he had got
into the habit as a result of Lugea's talkativeness or
whether it was a congenital defect could never be
decided.

Lugea finished his speech for him. "Of course
we're delighted. It's positively unnecessary to say so.
I can't bear superfluous words."

She was very dainty, that little Lugea, and well
she knew it. But of her own loquacity she had not
even the faintest suspicion. She did not even know
that she tyrannized over the worthy Klipps.

"Well, I declare," she chattered on, "there's Sitzer
over there. No, my dear, we don't have anything to
do with him now. He's such a rough. And do you
know," she bent quite close to Plana, "he has designs
on me. That's why he hates Klipps so. Oh, these
men! My dear, I tell you!" For a moment she was
still. "And that mussy person over there is Olva. No,
no, she doesn't live here. I'm sincerely thankful for

[168]

that. Just to think that she's in love with Klipps! What did you say?"

A pheasant interrupted the torrent of Lugea's talk.

He came in rapid flight from the direction in which the thunder was constantly pealing. He alighted very quickly, in the midst of the rabbits, so suddenly, and so little heedful of them, that they had to spring apart in order to make room for him.

As it was, his wings brushed Hops and Lugea. He did not notice them. He was no longer flying, he plunged when he was close above the ground. He had already lost consciousness and remained lying, his wings outspread, without stirring again.

The rabbits stared terrified at the inanimate creature that had carried its own death so far through the air.

Lugea wanted to begin chattering some sentimental nonsense.

But Hops commanded her sternly, "Keep quiet!" Lugea kept quiet.

Plana admired him.

Even Klipps and the others were grateful to him.

More pheasants flew in, fluttered down with outspread wings, which they then folded, and strutted about, sound and good-humored, like creatures that have just come safely through a great peril.

One pheasant whirred up and started to flutter as if his strength had failed him. He turned somersaults in the air and, tumbling over and over, plunged between the limbs of the trees, through the bushes to the ground. Ruffled almost beyond recognition, he lay still. It seemed to be all over with him. But after a while he stretched his neck, turned his little head and whispered, "Where am I?"

Then he rose, shook his feathers to rights and muttered, "Terrible, the way I look!" He ran a few steps, stopped, sank down. "I'm sick . . . ," he sighed to himself. "Odd, that it should be so sudden!" Again he rose, again ran a few steps, again stopped. "Pains," he murmured, "sharp pains . . ." He ran further as if he were in haste and vanished in the depths of the thicket.

A royal pheasant flew up proudly. His plumage was all splashed with gold and richly burnished, with white points. His long train was extremely imposing.

But he could not stand. He was shot through both feet. He had to lie on his breast. With all his splendor he made a sorry spectacle.

Then, as he touched the ground and sat on his wounded legs, he felt pierced by a burning pain. But he did not let anything be noticed. "I'm a little tired," he said quietly while the pain threatened to rend him to pieces.

"They won't get me," he thought, "not me."

When no one was looking, he crept on his belly into the deepest part of the thicket.

"We had better go farther on," Hops advised.

Plana was ready at once. "Yes, . . . anywhere where there are no horrible sights . . ."

Hops looked into her eyes. "Where is there such a place? Where in the whole forest are there no horrible sights?"

"But . . ." Plana pleaded, "but there's some happiness, too. . . ."

Hops raised his ears erect, and there was confidence in his bearing. "Yes, certainly. That's why we go on living! That's why we cling so to life."

They wandered through the evening twilight. It had become still after the uproar of the men.

As they passed through the undergrowth the pheasant, who had plunged down so abruptly, was sitting there. He was well hidden but breathing heavily.

They did not find the royal pheasant anywhere. Plana's heart was wrung.

Hops comforted her. "If no dog catches them— and no fox—they may get well again. . . ."

17

It began to snow again, this time in earnest. All day long, with very short pauses, the white flakes hovered down, soft, delicate, pure. They capered merrily through the air, as if it was never their intention, their purpose and their destiny to reach the ground. Or sometimes they would drive down in straight streaks, as though some simple childish hand were sketching in the colorless streaking of rain against the now colorless background of nature.

Soon the snow lay deep and heavy on the earth. It was all one because of the way it had fallen. It lay, exhaling its cold, and its layers grew, often from hour to hour, from one to two feet.

Flight became difficult; no creature in the forest could be as swift as before. The deer made leaps that carried them over the bushes. But their leaping lacked its former lightness. It took strength to pull their legs free of the cold, clinging mass. The frost pierced their slender limbs and they moved about less often.

To the rabbits the condition of the ground was a real calamity. They sank almost completely in the icy depth of the snow. Their beautiful easy running was impossible now. Even a long bound did not take them far forward. Then followed the soft, ineluctable sinking and they had to pluck up heart again for a new leap.

Hops and Plana sat quietly in the deep snow and nibbled the withered, frozen stems of the grasses. They were rather hungry at times, and at times felt a little faint. But Hops had discovered that as long as they kept still they were protected in the snow and that it was even warming, if they sat quiet.

"You're so clever, Hops," said Plana, snuggling up to him, "much cleverer than I am. I've found that out, too . . ."

"Stop it." Hops was pleased and at the same time embarrassed to be so praised.

They slept much of the time.

But Murk could not accommodate himself to the hard conditions. He wandered about restlessly, sought to vary the old paths to which he was accustomed, and which all lay under snow. He imagined that all the other rabbits were living very falsely and, in his unsettled mind, hoped to succeed in discovering the one true way. The snow pained him; his eyes smarted from its blinding whiteness, the cold disrupted his shattered nerves completely. He clung fast to the conviction that somewhere there must be fresh, green grass growing, juicy leaves, dry ground, sun, and warmth. It was only his longing for such abundance, which now amounted to madness, but he had fastened on this idea and could not be dislodged. Whenever the other rabbits saw him, his afflicted body and his manner, distorted by sorrow, grief and envy, gave them the impression that he had some important matter in hand, or some great secret.

In the course of one of his perpetual wanderings, Murk was suddenly stopped by some unknown obstacle and could not get away. In the midst of his struggles he felt a painful tug at his neck and had to lie down. He was terrified and bewildered and felt the impossibility of moving as long as that thin, hard loop was pressing into his neck.

He lay thoughtfully for a long while, pondering. What could it be?

How long would this new torment last?

He took the trap into which he had blundered to be one of the numerous accompaniments of winter, unpleasant but transient.

He waited patiently. Like the assurance with which a mortally sick man hopes for his recovery, a remarkable peacefulness came over Murk, for long intervals together. For the first time in months, he no longer felt afraid. The iron-like loop was cutting into his neck, but he waited, almost in high spirits and with mounting desire to live, for a miracle.

But the miracle did not happen.

"Well, it's high time now," thought Murk at last, "I probably ought to be going." He gave a bound which, of course, succeeded only in part. He fell back piteously, his neck strangling, fell, to his terrified astonishment, on his back. It was difficult for him to right himself again. With difficulty he forced the little breath remaining in him through his mouth and nose.

Time and time again Murk leaped, rallied all his strength and leaped—forward, backward, to the

side. The harder he leaped, the tighter grew the noose around his neck, the more cruelly it choked him.

Then such terror as he had never before known swept over him, a terror that quickly turned to desperation, and then to frenzy.

Murk sprang wildly, without method, without plan, almost without hope. He sprang into the air, simply for the sake of springing. He sprang because he was still living, because his whole heart was consumed with desire to live, and yet felt nothing but the imminence of death.

The snow grew powdery from the captive's leaps. When he fell to the ground the noose would slacken. But he would always leap into the air anew—and the noose would tighten.

A pair of crows passed by, Hops and Plana came, even Olva appeared. All stood around and watched solicitously as Murk struggled for his life against an incomprehensible, mysterious power.

Murk lay in the snow after the frenzy of his last terrified leaps. He lay on one side, almost unconscious, completely exhausted. The noose was choking him tighter than before. His eyes protruded, big and bloodshot, from his head. His breath came, whistling, short and labored; a bitter-tasting fever parched the roof of his mouth and tongue. He lay in a miserable kind of trance. His frenzy had barely diminished the terror he was suffering, and not at all the pain. In his trancelike condition the despair that overwhelmed him escaped him only in dull moans, as if from a distance, from somewhere else.

Faline, the mother doe, looked at the bush on which one branch shook violently whenever Murk jerked the noose.

"Poor thing," she whispered. "When I was still raising children, I lost a little son that way." She stopped. Then she said much more softly, "There's no escape from that."

She turned and went slowly away with the other deer. "I can't bear to look at it," she murmured.

The rabbits, too, withdrew, reluctantly, forbearingly, as one departs from someone who must not know that the leave-taking is final.

Murk remained alone. He lay quite still. He was sleeping, his breath rattling—the sleep of the exhausted.

When it was dark, Murk heard the step of the two-legged one, heard Him coming, nearer and nearer. Once more Murk made an effort, once more he attempted to escape, and, with all his senses now fully awake, once more suffered the most excruciating pain.

Then the forest heard his death shriek. It rose thin and wailing, like the terrible cry of some human child.

18

For several days a dog had been roaming around the forest. It was one of the pointers that He always took with Him when He hunted. There was much disquietude, much alarm, much fear and flight as a result of the presence of the dog.

Something unusual must have happened to him. They heard him whining softly to himself, heard him at times howl loudly and piteously. Then he would be silent again, and wander restlessly, his ears drooping, his tail between his legs, through the snow. He was very sad.

At first none of them put any faith in him. They

took all his strange actions for slyness and fled from him. But gradually it became quite apparent that this big, brown and black spotted dog, who looked so pitiable, meant well.

The squirrel ventured to speak to him. He came scampering down the huge beech-tree so fast that the snow was scattered from its branches. Inquisitively, his head cocked to one side, he rocked back and forth on the lowest branch, not sitting down, but ready at any moment to race up the limb.

"What's the matter with you?" exclaimed the squirrel.

The dog sat down on his haunches under the tree and wept softly. Then he looked up.

"Oh! you kind creature," he answered, "thank you for your question."

"You don't belong to us," cried the squirrel, growing bolder. "Leave us in peace."

The dog replied, "I want to belong to you . . . It would be better for me."

"Things are as they are," the squirrel said curtly.

"I do leave you in peace," the dog whimpered, "why don't you trust me?"

The squirrel began to insult him. "We know you and your kind."

"Only listen to me," pleaded the dog.

"Oh yes," said the squirrel. "I'll be glad to let you catch me!"

He bounded upward, twitching his tail. He remained sitting for a moment on a higher limb, peered down and vanished in a flash among the branches of his native tree.

It was not easy for the dog.

But the squirrel reported the conversation everywhere.

Pretty soon the fox, too, knew of the matter.

One night he had captured a wild duck, had dragged it into the thicket and was about to begin his meal. There was a crackling in the bushes; dull steps padded along, and in front of the fox stood the big, brown and black spotted dog who looked so pitiable. The fox waited for him, his head lowered, his lips drawn back in a threatening snarl.

"Give me that," the dog began at once.

"Catch one yourself," snapped the fox crossly.

"I'm so hungry," the dog said softly.

"So am I," barked the fox.

"But you're cleverer than I," the dog confessed, "you'll soon catch another."

The fox lay flat on the ground, his fore-paws tightly clutching the duck. Then he began to mock the dog. "What did you come into the forest for, you blockhead? Did you think for a moment that you could be free the way we are?"

"I will be free!" cried the dog with a piteous tone in his voice. "Free! Free!"

The fox looked him over contemptuously. "All your life long you've served Him," he said, "have betrayed us to Him. Do you understand for a moment what it means to be free? You fool! Go back to Him!"

The dog wagged his tail very feebly. "I want to be your comrade. After all, we're related."

"Go along with your 'related,'" growled the fox. "I've never yet had anything but annoyance from relatives. And now you want to take what's mine from me!"

Stiff-legged, the dog slowly drew near, his neck stretched out, his tail lifted straight and almost imperceptibly quivering. "For the last time," he growled deeply, "will you give it to me or not?"

The fox whisked to one side. "Thief," he hissed, "you cowardly robber! I won't fight you!"

The duck lay unguarded in front of the dog. He seized it greedily, buried his teeth in its still warm breast. Then he raised his head, his mouth full of bloody feathers. He shook himself and spat.

The fox began to laugh.

Again the dog bit into the duck, again and again, in the back, the neck, the wings. Finally he gave it up.

"I'll never be able to do it!" he sighed. "I've never done such a thing, never dared to do it. . . ."

"And *you* want to be free?" mocked the fox.

The dog grew faint. The taste of the raw flesh turned his stomach. The down that still stuck to his mouth and throat made him want to vomit. He sat down and let his tongue loll out.

He was quite helpless.

The fox crept forward cautiously. "If you'll permit me," he said sarcastically, and began to devour the duck, expertly, deliberately, with relish.

Watery saliva dripped from the dog's tongue as he looked on enviously. "I must learn to do that," he snapped, faint with hunger and nausea. "I'll learn to do it yet!"

"Well," the fox looked at him, "you've already killed enough . . ."

"Yes," the dog admitted, "plenty—rabbits, pheasants, partridges, even deer."

"Well then?" The fox was puzzled.

"Oh, they were all badly wounded. I simply found them. I just stopped their escape and gave them the finishing touches."

"And didn't you ever taste even a little of them yourself?"

"Never!" The dog held his head erect. "Never was I so forgetful of my duty," he said with conviction.

The fox blinked over at him. "You're still proud of it?"

"You don't understand such things," the dog answered loftily.

The fox laughed aloud. "No," he said, "I don't understand such things. Always to be putting yourself out for Him, always to be pursuing others for Him, betraying them, killing them, only for Him, never for yourself . . . No, I'm not stupid enough to understand that."

Both grew silent. After a while the fox began again. "What *do* you eat anyway?" He had finished with the duck by now and was satisfied. He licked his chops and felt in a comfortable humor, and inquisitive.

Hesitantly, embarrassedly, the dog explained. "I can eat only cooked food. All my life long I've eaten only cooked food. Now I'm old."

"What's that . . . cooked food?" the fox inquired.

The dog tried to explain the matter. "Meat that He roasts or stews on the fire in a pot." He grew more and more embarrassed.

[185]

Shaking his head, the fox said, "Fire . . . roasts . . . stews . . . pots . . . I've never heard of such things. I don't know what to make of it!"

The dog sprang up. "Now I'm going to live by myself!" he cried. "In the forest . . . like you! Free! Free!" He was beside himself. "I no longer believe in Him. I know now that He's bad . . ." But suddenly, shaken with grief, he wailed, "Yet in spite of that, in spite of that . . . I love Him! I love Him!"

"Why did you leave Him then, if you love Him?" inquired the fox.

"Because He was cruel to me!" All his woes burst forth at once. The dog told his troubles and his heart grew heavy in the process. The more he recalled his heart-ache the stronger grew his indignation. "My name is Iago," he said, "that's the name He gave me. Oh, He was kind to me, He was tender . . . He let me stay with Him, in His rooms."

"What are rooms?" the fox demanded.

The dog kept right on talking. "But since the other has been there," he moaned, "the young one, since He's had Treff, He's changed! Now it's only Treff who gets petted! He kicks me away with His foot! Only Treff is allowed to stay with Him, I have to sleep outside in the cold! When that beastly

Treff attacked me, and I wanted to defend myself against him, I got beaten for it! Only I! But I couldn't stand the torture, the agony! I can't stand it! It's too cruel, too cruel!" He fastened his despairing eyes on the fox. "Why is it? Why is it? Because I'm old now, and Treff is young?"

The fox had risen and drew nearer. "Everything you tell me is so strange," he said, "I don't understand a word. What is . . . a beating?"

Stammering, the dog informed him.

The fox's eyes flashed, "And you didn't leap at His throat?"

Iago was horrified. "At Him? At Him?" he cried. "How can you even think of such a thing? Don't you know that He is all-powerful?"

The fox walked slowly around Iago and snuffed him carefully. "You smell strange," he said calmly, "strange and bad. You're different from us. Anyone who can take a beating, anyone who can submit to a beating as something natural, will never be free!"

"I won't submit any longer," howled the dog. "I've run away from Him."

"Run back to Him again," cried the fox, "run home again. You'll never be able to live among free creatures!"

The dog pulled himself together. "Oh, you," he said, "you're simply jealous of me . . . because I was with Him."

"Your mistake," answered the fox. "If I didn't despise you so much, I'd have to pity you."

He turned his back and walked off. The dog followed him and wanted to seize him. But the fox swished his bushy tail in the dog's face, uttered a wild, scornful howl and slipped away.

Iago stood bewildered, rubbed his face and muzzle in the snow, shook himself and muttered, "I'll succeed! I've got to succeed!"

He immediately began to rummage around for prey. A gnawing hunger spurred him on, and a last flare-up of defiance.

It was Hops and Plana whom he frightened out of their beds.

When they heard him coming, panting loudly, on padding feet, Hops whispered, "He isn't dangerous! Running away will be a game with him."

So it proved. Both rabbits fled apart, in opposite directions. Iago twisted around. Then he followed Plana, who ran in a circle that made him dizzy. He gave Plana up and set out after Hops, who had immediately challenged him to leave Plana. But Hops' tricks were mysteries to Iago. After a while he felt himself completely worn out. The rabbits had disappeared.

The dog remained alone.

He thought of his master with a longing that caused him bitter pain, with reproaches that failed to afford him any solace, but only a yearning that kept intensifying.

He thought of all the free creatures in the forest who despised him. He had tried to be a comrade to them, but it was only his homelessness and humiliation that impelled him.

A wild homesickness overcame him.

"What am I to do in this world?" he cried, and his outcry echoed lonely in the stillness of the night.

19

The snow had frozen hard so that it crunched in the forest. It cracked on the branches of the trees when a squirrel whisked over it or a bird hopped from limb to limb.

The noise kept the rabbits' nerves in a state of continual terror. They were constantly afraid that some marauder was slinking up.

But in the fields they lay in the furrows and hollows, could hear instantly whatever was approaching in the distance, had but to raise their ears quickly or sit up on their hind-legs, and they could always see the danger threatening them, even from afar. Sometimes, at midday, they enjoyed the soft caresses of the pale sun. Yes, the sun could still shine warmly now and again. Then the rabbits grew more confident and scraped among the clods for a little food. But soon those pleasant hours passed, too. The frost set in still worse.

Hops and Plana were sitting in the middle of the field.

The forest ranged far beyond them, and its black and white wall of trees and bushes made a level arc halfway around the vast, snow-covered flat plain. On the farther side, the roofs of the houses in the village were visible, with the church spire towering above them. The rabbits, not knowing exactly what these structures might signify, paid little attention to them.

Plana twitched the fur on her back; she was impatient. "I wonder if it will ever be the way it was before?" she sighed.

Hops wiggled his whiskers. "What do you mean . . . ?"

"Oh!" Plana grew ecstatic. "Oh, everything green . . . The days warm . . . warm at night . . . singing in the trees. And wonderfully good things everywhere, delicious things, more than you need . . . many, many more . . . I wonder if it will ever come again?"

Hops sat upright. "I think . . . I believe it will be that way again."

Plana closed her eyes, overwhelmed by her recollection. "Oh! that was a happy time!"

"Yes," Hops agreed, "it certainly was. Now the times are hard. But they predicted it."

"Who?"

"The old folks."

"Yes," Plana had lost her brief enthusiasm, "but they didn't say that good times will surely come back, did they?"

Hops, too, let his ears drop. But he wanted to say something comforting and murmured, "Well, in any case, we'll just have to wait."

"Do you remember how glorious it was out here in the fields?"

"Don't think about it now; it simply makes you sad."

Plana brushed her fore-paws across her face. "We can't imagine it anymore as things are . . ."

Hops stiffened; his ears and whiskers twitched.

Crouched low, Plana asked, "What is it?"

Hops remained erect. "I don't know, but something's wrong."

"Danger?"

Still erect, Hops replied, "I don't know . . . so many rabbits are running . . ."

"Are they rabbits we know?" Plana was curious, but she did not stir.

"No, they're absolute strangers." Hops was excited. "Strange how they run this way and that."

"It's no concern of ours," said Plana, but she, too, grew excited.

Hops looked farther afield. "They are so far away." He wanted to give the appearance of calm. "It's hard to tell whether we know any of them or not."

"Lie down," Plana begged. His alertness worried her. "Lie down again."

Hops was about to obey.

Suddenly a string of partridges whirred over, rustling close to the ground, and they heard the low warning, "Save yourselves!"

They were gone again.

Then, from the other side a second string of partridges whirred up, soaring high in the air. They uttered the same warning.

Hops and Plana stood as if they had been jerked to their feet. They turned bewilderedly in circles.

Then they saw that the whole vast field had become alive with swarming, leaping rabbits.

"What shall we do? What shall we do?" wailed Plana.

"I don't understand it at all," Hops stammered.

Suddenly his mother ran by in wild flight.

"Mother!" Hops called. "Mother!"

The old mother rabbit checked herself and nearly tumbled head over heels. Then she sat down, breathing heavily.

"Mother," Hops pleaded, "which way shall we run?"

"Away!" she panted. "Away!" And remained sitting there. Her flanks were trembling.

Stout old Fosco came galloping along and sat down beside Hops' mother.

"Horrible!" he panted. "Horrible!"

"But what is it?" Hops and Plana asked together.

"The worst there is. The very worst," he declared.

"Fly! Fly!" commanded Hops, taking courage at his own decision.

"Impossible!" Fosco replied in a hopeless tone.

Hops' mother turned and turned, raised her ears and let them fall. Her silence bore witness to her despair.

Rabbits kept running incessantly across the field. Their dark, streaking bodies shot back and forth in confused lines across its white surface.

Ivner and Mamp rushed up; Nella and Olva joined them. A pair of strangers halted by the group.

Mamp attempted to jest. "The whole tribe has gone crazy . . ." he said, "and as nearly as I can see I have, too."

"The time for joking is past," Fosco reprimanded him.

Then the thunder crashed, cracked and crackled as if to confirm Fosco's words.

Although the noise was far off, and the report reached them very faintly, all the rabbits began to tremble.

From afar they saw the fire flash from the mouths of many guns; then they heard a peal that seemed to tear the air to shreds.

Hops turned in the opposite direction. "Come, Plana," he said dully. "Come! this way!"

"Stop," Fosco commanded.

At the same time the fiery mouths spurted on that side, too.

Then the rabbits saw that they were surrounded. On every side danger crashed and thundered at them; everywhere flashed the sharp, little flames that preceded the thunder.

Lugea, Klipps and Sitzer rushed by. Lugea began

at once. "I'm beside myself! What haven't I been through! What haven't I seen! How can I describe it to you . . . ?"

Fosco interrupted her gruffly. "Don't describe anything, and don't chatter!"

Lugea wanted to feel outraged, wanted to retort with something cutting, but she perceived that they were in very little humor for it. She kept silent.

Fosco gave counsel and orders. No one had ever seen the old fellow so agitated, but everyone admired how he kept hold, how he controlled himself.

"We must go through the thunder," he said, and his voice was almost calm; they could hear only a slight tremor in it. "We must go through the midst of the thunder." He stopped, for he could not go on. "Wait! Wait," he added after a few moments, "there's no sense in exhausting ourselves yet. But when the right moment comes, it means running with all your strength, running like the wind . . . not close together . . . everyone for himself!"

"That's what Trumer always said," Hops whispered to Plana. "Everyone for himself!"

"We must pass very close to the thunder," Fosco said. "Only swiftness and cunning can save you."

Hops' mother stood up; her eyes traveled about

the group. "Many of us are dying now," she said with an effort, "many of us will die today before we flee. I want to say farewell to you . . ."

Incessantly He banged, clattered, clamored with His mysterious thunder-arms, and drew constantly nearer.

Presently the little group saw how, far off, at the edge of the field, He started up by the hundred. He spread around them in a circle. But not all of Him had thunder-arms. There were five or six who simply carried sticks.

The little group saw, too, how many rabbits spun around on their heads after the crashing salvoes, tumbled head over heels, the whites of their bellies showing, kicking until they lay motionless.

Here and there, on the outside of the circle, they observed dogs that sprang upon the wounded rabbits. The fallen creatures tried to get to their feet and slip away. Then a dog would overtake them, seize them in his jaws, and the piteous death-screams of the poor creatures would horrify the terror-stricken survivors.

Fosco sat stiffly erect, his ears lifted high, his whole body quivering with readiness to flee.

Hops kept close to Plana and remained silent.

All the rabbits as they sat together were trembling in mortal fear and with feverish anticipation of flight.

Mamp, the jovial, was the first to lose heart. His face fell from moment to moment. He became restless and ran to and fro frantically. Suddenly he began to gallop straight up to the circle that He was drawing tighter and tighter.

Fosco called after him, "Not along the line of beaters!"

But Mamp did not heed him. For a moment he did not even heed himself. He had forgotten all his tricks, all his cunning. He was frantic with the agony of fear, frantic with desire to escape. As he approached the deafening thunder, his consciousness and his purpose faded. Blindly he ran along the line of fire, ran on, driven by the dully throbbing hope that somewhere it would not crash.

Four times Mamp spun head over heels. His bloody head dyed the snow red. Disfigured and dead, he lay for a moment on his back, then rolled over gently on his side.

His comrades watched. Horror gripped them.

"He faced it," said Hops' mother sadly, "now it's our turn."

Lugea could be restrained no longer. She carried Klipps and the utterly despondent Nella along with her. They rushed forward quite close together.

"Separate!" Fosco commanded them, "separate!"

"Keep quiet, you old fool," Lugea flung back.

The next minute she spun over on her head, fell with a touchingly gentle gesture that was not at all like her, and did not stir again.

Klipps rolled over and over, lithe and elastic, as if he were performing a feat. He raised his head again and crawled forward painfully on his belly. No one noticed him.

Nella dropped as if she had been struck by lightning. Like a stunned fly, she remained on the spot where she was hit and died instantly.

Then something strange occurred.

A dog appeared in the middle of the circle and ran the length of the fire-spurting line. He was in the greatest danger.

The thunder ceased wherever the dog appeared.

Everywhere the dog went He burst into shouts, abuse and curses.

Hops, who hung passionately on Fosco's words, had recovered his clear head and decisive firmness. He perceived the opportunity; he comprehended that it was less dangerous to keep close to the dog.

"Come, Plana," he whispered, turned to his mother and whispered, "Come now, mother."

Then he ran. "Farewell, my Plana," he thought at the same time. "Farewell, dear mother." But he did not say anything. He simply called to Plana, "Keep close to the dog! To the dog!"

Plana followed him at once.

His mother hesitated.

"Shall I . . . ?" she asked Fosco.

"Perhaps he's right . . ." he answered. "I can't tell you anything better now."

Hops and Plana scampered almost between the dog's legs. They did not recognize him. They were in too frantic haste.

They heard how He shouted, "Iago! Come here! You damned runaway! Iago! Iago!"

But they understood nothing of it. The roaring terrified them, for it was very close.

Then they broke through. They were already free, and fled like mad through the forest.

Iago howled under the blows of the whip, cowered on the ground and was kicked.

The two fugitives heard his tortured voice. "Have mercy!" they heard. "Have mercy! I am old! I beg you to have mercy!"

It was still ringing in their upraised ears when they reached the protecting thicket.

They remained, sitting breathless. Their hearts were pounding against their ribs which were sticky wet. It leaped almost into their parched mouths. It hammered in their buzzing temples. But Hops and Plana looked at each other and were happy.

"The poor thing . . ." Plana said finally.

Then the thunder crashed again, crashed and crackled sharper than before.

Hops remembered. "Where is mother?" he asked.

"Your mother?" Plana answered anxiously. "I haven't seen her."

"Wasn't she behind us?" asked Hops, worried.

"I don't know."

Hops started up suddenly, shouting, "Here she comes!"

True enough, his mother came bounding up, trailing a little cloud of powdered snow behind her. When she reached the thicket, she stopped for a moment. "So you're saved, my dearest son!" she said in a panting voice. "I'm so glad! I'm so glad!" She rushed away immediately.

"Mother," Hops begged, "rest for a little while! Only for a little!"

"Impossible," she answered as she ran. "Never mind me! We'll see one another again!" She was gone.

Afterwards Hops and Plana found drops of blood along his mother's trail.

Outside, meanwhile, the circle had grown narrower. The less dangerous He, who carried only sticks, had retired. Only those with the thunder-arms remained. They were raging horribly among the rabbits.

At the very last minute, when the circle had grown very tiny, and every moment within it meant certain death, a huge old hare leaped out of it. The thunder crashed behind him, the snow spurted up under the driving hail of buckshot. But the old hare reached the forest uninjured. It was Fosco.

The evening began to darken, a mournful gray. Soon night fell, not completely dark, for the snow glistened too brightly.

Here and there, faint and pathetic, sounded the last cry of some wounded rabbit, that had lain silent in its agony and now was being killed. Fox and weasel were picking up the crumbs.

Deep in the forest Hops and Plana were sitting beside Fosco.

In a troubled voice Hops told about his mother.

"Where can she be?" he asked plaintively. "What can have become of her?"

"Don't worry about her," Fosco comforted him. "Believe me, she is not badly off."

But there was no comforting Hops. "If one of our enemies attacked her . . ."

"None of them will ever find her," Fosco assured him, "none of them! Your mother is very clever! Very clever! It would be difficult even for me to find her!"

"How did you manage to escape, Fosco?" Plana changed the conversation.

"I don't know myself," he answered.

"It was a dreadful day," sighed Plana.

Fervently Hops agreed, "An unforgettably terrible day!"

Fosco was silent for a while. Then he said softly and thoughtfully, "The life-time of a rabbit lasts seven years—eight at most. And while it is beautiful, it is also full of terror and flight . . . Be happy that you are alive, my children!"

20

Outside on the fields it grew more silent than ever. Many of the rabbits were now afraid to venture out on that vast, white expanse. For days the terrible hecatomb was written on the snow in letters of spattered red. As far as the enormously broad, snow-laden fields extended, the soaked-in, sprinkled blood stood out sharply on the glistening white surface, admonishing, recalling and distilling an acrid smell into the cold air. The horror of that day had given place to a dull sorrow. None of the rabbits said a word about the terrors they had been through, no one mentioned the fallen. Only, when two of them chanced to meet, even if they had not known one another before, or perhaps but very slightly, they greeted cordially. In the lively wiggling of their ears, in the violent twitching of their whiskers, all the joy of the saved lay unspoken.

Then the snow fell again, blotting the bloody traces from the white expanse, veiling the episode forever. Among the rabbits a vague feeling grew stronger, that from now on He would leave them in peace. At the same time their need for food grew catastrophically, drove them, in spite of everything, into the open fields, and from the fields back to the forest. It was incredible, all that the rabbits ate at that time in order not to starve. They gnawed wood, they munched withered leaves, they chewed dry tufts of frozen grass. These even seemed exceptional delicacies to them.

The winter wore on. It grew bitter cold, and the rabbits had to preserve the little of their own decreasing warmth that remained to them.

Hops and Plana had found a little spot in the forest. There the wind had swept the ground clean of snow. There were roots, little dry twigs, remnants of all sorts of things, of lettuce and strawberry leaves. Everything that had once been flourishing, filled with fragrance, sap and tastiness, was now frozen solid, watery and poisonously bitter. Though he struggled against it manfully, Hops was overcome with nausea.

"Eat very little," he said, "just as little as is absolutely necessary . . . eat very little!"

Plana had never been as cheerful as at present. Of course, it was not really a genuine, but often an assumed, cheerfulness, yet it helped both of them over the worst places.

"Let's run," she would propose. "Let's run, Hops! That makes you warm!"

So they would run, in little circles, bouncing one after the other as in their childhood days.

"Catch me, Hops," she would cry and rush away, Hops after her.

"I'll get you," he would threaten jestingly. "I'll catch you in a minute!"

But things were not as before; their once rapid movements were feeble. They would soon sit down again, tired out; they had grown short-winded. They panted, their flanks heaved.

"Hard times!" the worried Hops complained.

"What of it?" Plana retorted. "They'll pass. The hard times will soon go. It's nothing after all."

"Nothing?" Hops was doubtful. "Suppose we go first . . . ?"

Plana's ears flew up. "We go? My Hops talking like that? My clever, determined Hops?"

"No," he objected, "I'm no longer clever, and I'm no longer determined."

Plana bounced close up to him. Her whiskers quivered tenderly; her ears lay flat along her back. "What's the matter with you? Are you sick?"

Hops winced a little under the blow her question gave him. He looked at Plana. She was as pretty as a picture, but she looked emaciated, poorly. She was touching and careworn. But her maiden grace moved him the more powerfully.

"I?" he stammered. "I . . . am all right, but my fear for you torments me."

"You needn't fear for me," Plana went on proudly. "You have no reason to think so for a single moment. Come, come along!"

She sprang away. Hops went after her and they tumbled over each other, so that a cloud of white powder hid them.

"Enough," Hops begged, breathless.

"No," Plana answered, "not by a long shot. You're too lazy for me."

She danced and tumbled about as though she were perfectly fresh. "Catch m . . ." Then she sank over her ears in a drift of loose snow. Suddenly she was no longer there.

Hops stood up, surprised, on his hind-legs, staring in alarm, his ears erect.

Plana was kicking free. The snow spurted up in a powder around her. Slowly she made her appearance again, gasped for breath, tried to speak. "It's jolly . . ." she managed to say. Then she lay down, stretched at full length, quite still and breathing hard. She was completely exhausted.

Hops sat beside her and muttered, "You see! You see!"

She comforted him in an almost toneless voice.

In the meanwhile, however, it grew steadily worse.

The cold set in sharper and sharper. The air seemed to be perfectly thin and as clear as glass. And, like brittle glass, the stems of the bushes, that had once been so pliant and elastic, broke in two at the slightest touch.

The deer sank up to their necks in snow, were no longer able to clear it by the momentum of their leaping, and here and there they could be heard complaining in the forest.

Even the elk pushed their way through with difficulty; everywhere they gnawed the bark from the trees.

There were nights when the forest grew rigid in the icy grip of winter, and seemed dead. At such times flight was difficult for the birds when they awoke in the morning. Their plumage was caked with ice and would not buoy them up; their legs were stiff.

The snow was very hard and coated with ice. When a deer walked or leaped over it, the icy covering would give way. Then its splinters slashed the deer's tender feet. There were many deer limping around with bloody legs. The cold burnt like hot fire into their torn flesh.

In silence the winter reigned, without storms, without changing humors. Pitiless, stubborn, cruel, annihilating, silent.

The wild-geese flew farther on to more southerly, milder stretches of the sky. The wild ducks followed them, and all kinds of arctic birds that were trying to escape the polar winter and had been overtaken by it. The river courses were frozen many feet deep; the pools and ponds were ice to the bottom, so that all living things in them perished miserably.

The frost began to hum in the air. It was a lingering whine, like a lament, like a song for the dead. At night the fox would bark at it and howl from hunger, and still more from the cold.

But a time came when the fox was almost harmless. No one was afraid of him. For suddenly there was food in plenty. Everywhere in the forest lay rabbits and deer, rigid, frozen to death. Even a young elk was found stretched out one morning on its white bed. The fighting of flocks of crows and fluttering magpies would always indicate the occurrence of such an event.

"That pack is always provided for," said Hops, gasping with the cold. "They can turn everything to advantage."

"What do you expect?" answered Plana. "They are strong. They have no dislike for our blood . . ."

Hops sighed. "And we have to help them out, have to give our lives so that crew can survive the winter. And afterwards they murder us all the more skillfully."

Plana shook her pretty head. "We are poor . . ."

"It isn't right," Hops said. "Things are not well managed in this world . . . it's easy to become embittered . . ."

"Embittered! Why?" Plana was astonished. "Just think how radiantly beautiful the world is! Just remember!"

Hops sat up. He had not heard what Plana said. He sat erect and tense. "Do we really have to stand for it? If we could get together, we rabbits and all the deer, all the oppressed and the hunted! If we were to get together . . ."

It was night, and the cold bit into their lungs, into their bones, took away their breath, stuck in their throats.

Plana grew sick at heart.

"Come!" She bounded up. "Come, let's have another race."

Hops refused. "I won't run. I'll just sit here."

"But you must," Plana interrupted, "it keeps you warm."

She ran. She hardly noticed at first that Hops was not following her. She ran straight on until the forest lay behind her, and she came to the open fields. Then she perceived that she was alone. But she ran on.

She felt weak, strangely tired, and experienced a great longing simply to lie down and sleep. For that very reason she ran on in a remarkable state of semi-consciousness at the bottom of which lurked desperation. A supreme danger was threatening her. Plana sensed it vaguely; only she did not know just what it was.

She did not know, either, that she was running more and more slowly. On the contrary, it seemed to her as if she had never run so fast before, for she was exerting all her strength and had to make a tremendous effort.

Presently the fields, too, lay behind her. She had penetrated into a strange world.

In a garden surrounded by a fence a small house was standing. A lamp was burning behind the curtained window, casting a soft gleam into the dark.

Plana had never seen anything like it before.

She was running with the slight wind, so she smelt no scent when she stopped, stood up on her hind-legs and snuffed.

Only the biting, icy air rasped her nose and the top of her mouth. Everything pained her, her legs, breast, belly, neck. Everything in her was quivering and longing for a little warmth, a little rest.

Plana tottered forward.

Suddenly she realized: He was there.

But she was not frightened. Vaguely she felt her need as a kind of protection. Vaguely, as through a mist, she felt it was her right to come even to Him. She could not think; everything was one to her now.

As she slipped through the fence and hopped forward painfully, she came upon an unfamiliar sight! A dog-house!

Plana stopped short. But even then she was not

frightened as she snuffed in the poisonously bitter scent of the dog. The scent was pouring out of the opening in the front of the kennel, which was curtained with rags. It smelt warm.

Plana did not stop to consider: she found herself in a state where all her old instincts and fears were numbed.

Warmth! Warmth! That was all she sought . . . And warmth came pouring out of the kennel.

Plana shoved her nose among the rags that hung before the opening. They yielded and she crept in.

Had she, in her state of half-frozen exhaustion, been capable of thinking at all, she would have thought this the luckiest hour of her life. But at first she could not even speak. Noiselessly she sank down on the silken soft, deliciously warm straw; breathed in, wonderfully refreshed, the tepid air that filled the narrow place with vapor, and snuggled against the strong, warm body of the dog, who awoke at her entrance.

"Ha! How cold you are!" whispered the dog, at the same time beginning to lap Plana with his long, warm tongue.

Plana lay without stirring. The smell of the dog, that had formerly seemed menacing and repulsive to her, as to all the other rabbits, did not disturb her in the slightest now. The thought that she might be bitten to death presented itself as usual, but only vaguely, and, for some strange reason, held no terrors for her. Plana lay quiet, enjoying the caresses of that long, warm tongue on her back, her flanks, her face, her ears. It was wonderful, it was exactly what she needed, it was the reviving sense of life.

"You poor thing, you!" whispered the dog. "You poor little thing! Are you still cold?" He continued lapping her without stopping.

Plana was quite damp; her fur clung all over her body in thick strings. Her whole body began to steam. Full of a blissful comfort, she snuggled up close to the dog's chest.

"Yes, yes," said the dog and passed his tongue over her eyes. "Yes, you, you trust me; of all the creatures out there in the forest, you alone trust me . . ."

Plana was in a delicious semi-conscious state; she hardly heard what the dog was saying.

"I received you more kindly," he said, "more kindly than you in the forest received me—old Iago . . ."

The name had a familiar ring. "Iago?" she asked softly. "Iago?"

"Of course," the dog answered, "of course, I'm Iago."

Plana was about to confess, "I didn't know that," but she suddenly fell asleep.

The dog didn't notice and told her his story. The contempt with which they had repulsed his attempts at reconciliation in the forest had driven him home again. Added to that, of course, was his hunger, the cold and the unaccustomed, strange ways of a free life. The rabbit hunt had overtaken him. He was cut off with the rabbits and partridges, without knowing it. Think of what his bewilderment had been! Think of his terrible dilemma—love, longing drove him to his master; fear, jealousy and his injuries held him back. He ran aimlessly around the wide circle, regretting his whole life, desperate.

At last his master had called him. At last! Joyful but afraid, he had rushed up to Him.

Oh! what a beating he received, what a murderous beating!

But it was a shorter one than usual. His master could not spare much time for Iago. And most remarkable of all—his beating, his reunion with Him, his decision, everything together had strengthened Iago. He suddenly felt strong, serious and brave. He immediately settled accounts with his enemy, Treff. Towards the end of the hunt, when Treff was far from his master, on the trail of a wounded rabbit, Iago fell upon him.

Recalling all his old rough-house tricks, Iago threw the astonished Treff violently on his back in the snow. Raging with long restrained fury, Iago had pressed Treff down, held him by the throat and snarled, "I'll kill you, you scoundrel, if you make a sound! I'll kill you, you blackguard, if you don't let me alone in the future!" Whining feebly, Treff had promised everything.

Plana awoke just as Iago reached the end of his story. Shortly after, she heard him say, "So, you see, little one, now I am left in peace, at least . . ."

But Plana, who was stretching luxuriously, was hungry, with a gnawing, rumbling hunger.

"Come outside with me," Iago suggested, "my dish is still half full. Perhaps you'll find something . . ."

They crept out of the kennel. It was still dark, and the cold gripped them with redoubled sharpness. However, in Iago's bowl there were several boiled potatoes, for he had eaten only the meat from his supper.

Plana tried a potato. It tasted strange, but it tasted good. It had a scent that was disagreeable, but Plana's hunger overcame that. She ate greedily. She gorged herself as she had been unable to gorge herself for a long time.

The dog stood beside her, wagging his tail.

Then they both slipped into the dog-house again.

"Thanks," said Plana, "thanks, that was wonderful."

She hurried back among the straw. Iago followed her, and they both slept, side by side, until broad daylight.

Presently He came out to the dog-house.

"Iago!" He called. "Iago!"

But Iago simply pointed his ears. He did not get up.

Plana awoke and trembled when His scent penetrated to her.

"Be calm," Iago said to her, "don't be afraid . . . I'll protect you."

In front of the dog-house He said, "I'll have to see what's happened to the dog!" He raised the rags that covered the entrance. His pale face appeared in the opening.

But Iago snarled at Him, his teeth bared, so that He shrank back afraid.

"Well, well," they heard Him mutter. Then He went away. On the threshold of His house He told someone, "Iago has a rabbit in there with him and he's guarding it." As if he were stopping someone from looking, He added, "Don't, let the two of them be!"

It was the first time that Iago had ever growled at Him or showed his teeth.

Perhaps He sensed something of the reconciling mystery of need in whose profound power it lies to extinguish, for brief whiles, the enmity among creatures.

All day long Plana lay in the warm kennel. All day long the dog watched over her, lapping her constantly with his warm, affectionate tongue.

But when evening set in Plana suddenly sprang into the open and sat upright, her ears erect. She felt wonderfully fresh, and it seemed to her as if it were even warm outside. At first she believed it was an illusion. A sweet intoxication clouded her senses. Again and again she let her ears drop, then raised them quickly, her whiskers quivering with growing excitement.

Actually! A gentle breeze stirred the air, so softly and tenderly that Plana was oppressed with a feeling of anxiousness, of joy and longing.

"Come back in!" the dog called to her.

But she was already running across the snow

towards the forest, running through the melting snow, swiftly, without stopping, as if in flight.

"Hops," she thought as she ran, "my Hops!" Only that. Nothing else.

It was the last cold night of the winter.

21

Among the other trees in the forest stood a group of birches. They had grown up together, had struggled for room for their roots, for their place in the sun and air. Now they stretched up tall, and the mottled silver of their bark glistened, discernible from far off, amidst the ashes, elms and oaks. Their branches were still bare, like all the other branches in the once leafy forest. But up from the earth, from the depths of the nourishing soil, the sap was beginning to mount and swell, was, despite the cold, reviving the living flesh of the wood, while the birches waited with the rest of the trees to whom something similar was happening.

Only one of them felt downcast and feeble. Her branches looked strangely black, were quite dry, and several times limbs snapped off when a squirrel scampered along, or a pheasant lighted on them.

"Are you sick?" her sisters asked the birch.

"I don't know what's the matter with me," she answered. But the reply cost her an effort; her voice sounded changed.

Then she grew silent. All day and all night long she stood among her whispering sisters, sorrowful and mute.

Now and again, one or another of the birches would inquire, "Well, how are you?"

"Always about the same," she would sigh.

Once she said quite of her own accord, "I'll probably never have leaves again," then, in a hushed tone, "never again . . ."

The others comforted, soothed and encouraged her. "Wait till the sun comes again . . ."

"I am waiting," she said softly. But still more softly she whispered, "The sun can't help me anymore . . . even if I live to see it . . ."

But the warm breezes suddenly increased, blew up into a storm. The storm grew and became a hurricane. It raged across the land from the south, blew from the African desert, sped across the sunny Mediterranean and seemed bent, like a mad thing, on ending the icy misery. It came as a rebel, an insurgent, a liberator. Its onslaughts released the forest from the grip of its winter rigidity, snatched from the fields and meadows the shroud under which they had been sleeping. Its flaming jaws devoured the snow. The tread of its burning feet trampled it to nothing; its fiery hands swept away everything white and cold with their swift and angry touch. In a few hours its fury had snapped the icy fetters of the lakes and streams, the rivers and brooks, so that they broke free, with a crash like thunder, and everywhere was a roaring, crashing, leaping and brawling of waters, plunging once more into motion.

In the howling of the hurricane no one heard the feeble voice of the sick and frozen birch.

"I'll never be able to endure it," she groaned, "it's beyond my strength."

But all the trees in the forest were groaning, moaning, crackling and cracking under the terrible blasts of the hurricane-liberator. Stout branches split from many of them and were carried down like feathers. The sound trees resisted as, flexible and full of the mounting sap, they writhed and twisted, only to spring back again a moment later. The sound trees understood the revolt that was taking place against the winter's tyranny. There were a few firm, old trees, and many young ones, eager for life, who answered the terrible blasts exultantly.

When the sick birch died, no one heard her, not even her sisters who stood close around.

"Oh! how alone I am," she cried with her last breath. "Can I really be so utterly alone . . . !"

Then she snapped, close above the ground. "Farewell, my roots," she breathed in falling, "farewell . . . and many thanks."

The hurricane flung herself against an ash, tore the dead limbs from among its living branches, and hurled the silver-shimmering dead things hard against the earth. There they lay, with nothing left to show they had existed but a short, white, splintered stump that would slowly turn gray and rotten. Later the roots thrust thin little shoots, with tender leaves, out of the stump. Their appearance touched all the trees and bushes.

22

The earth had drunk the flood of thawing waters. It had grown sleek and black with them. It lay like a joyous hope, with its bare fields, its bare woods standing darkly. A mysterious ferment was going on everywhere, invisible and noiseless, was going on so passionately, with such elemental force, that had anyone heard it he would have likened it to the storm with which spring had come roaring in. This ferment was taking place in the earth, in the roots and branches of the trees, in the tangled stems of the thicket, in the tilled fields. It had its echo in the

hearts of all living creatures. It was reviving life itself.

A morning dawned fair and splendid, with a golden sun. The light blue sky arched overhead and seemed higher, purer than ever in the radiant and joyous color with which it blessed the world.

No one knew when it happened, and yet everyone thought he had seen it, believed, at least in secret, that he had actually seen it—but toward midday the trees and bushes were no longer black, were no longer bare. A delicate, light-green shimmer outlined the gray contours of the tree-tops. Big and little branches no longer stretched out, as though destitute and desperate, into the air. All were now adorned by life itself.

The earth in the forest and in the fields was clad in the same delicate shimmer; it did not yet quite venture to be green, but it was an exquisite, renascent yellow.

A marvelous singing was welling up everywhere, inaudible, or audible only to the soul. The clods sang, the trees sang, the tiniest blade of grass sang as it sprouted towards the light. Then the voices of the birds chimed in, voices that had so long been mute. First the blackbirds rejoiced from the highest tips of the highest trees. Then came purling down those magic sounds that the lark flings high above the fields. Then the oriole fluted his genial message of joy, incessantly, through the forest. The whispering of the titmice sounded again, the throbbing call of the finches, the mocking cry of the woodpecker and his cheery drumming.

A royal pheasant strutted haughtily through the vast festival. He limped a little but concealed it cleverly, and the splendor of his appearance was only slightly impaired.

"Well, well," said Plana, "so you are about again?"

"Thanks," he replied with morose majesty, "everything is quite all right."

"Congratulations!" laughed Hops.

The royal pheasant took a few steps, stopped and asked haughtily, "Can one notice anything at all . . . ?"

"Nothing," Hops hastened to reply.

Plana added quickly, "No, you can't notice anything at all. We remembered you from that time, well, you know when . . . it looked serious then . . ."

"A little misfortune," the royal pheasant said, pompously, "hardly worth mentioning." Without a farewell, he strutted off, limping.

"We ought to have told him that he limps dreadfully," said Plana.

"Why?"

Her whiskers quivered violently. "Oh, because he's so conceited and unfriendly."

"Let him be what he wants to," said Hops, "beautiful but stupid, according to my way of thinking. We don't want to spoil the pleasure of any living thing."

Plana let her one ear droop so that it hung far down beside her neck. The other lay on her back. "Do you suppose I could have told the conceited fool the truth? No, I love him even if he is conceited and a fool. I love everything that lives!"

Hops sat in front of her, his ears bolt upright. "Even me?" he wanted to know.

But instead of answering, Plana ran away.

Hops rushed after her. They tumbled over one another. Then they sat side by side.

"I'm so happy," whispered Plana.

Hops rested his head in his fore-paws. He had become serious. "If I knew where my mother was," he murmured, "I'd be the happiest rabbit in the forest. I don't even know if she's still alive."

Plana sprang up. "Come, let's look for her . . ."

They had not long to look. At the edge of the thicket, near their own native meadow, his mother was sitting, sunning herself.

Fosco was beside her.

"Mother!" cried Hops. "Mother!"

He nudged her flank with his nose and rubbed his whiskers against her fur, for he did not want anyone to see his tears.

"Well," said his mother comfortingly, "well, well, well . . ."

Plana went up to the older rabbit and said quickly, "Tell us how long you were sick, mother, and where you hid yourself. Tell us."

"One doesn't talk about such things," Fosco declared, gently but firmly. A silence followed. Then he turned to Hops' mother. "We must be going," he said. "Come!"

He bounded off.

"Goodbye, my children," said Hops' mother gently, "may everything go well with you." And she followed her companion.

"We won't let it go badly," laughed Plana.

"No," Hops laughed, too. "Only . . . don't eat any leeks!" he warned her.

Plana made an astonished face. "My dear fellow," she said, "haven't you anything better to say to me than that?"

Hops crept up close to her. "That before everything else," he insisted. "I want you to keep in good health."

Plana grew happier and happier. "There are so many good things, so many good things are sprouting every day . . . why should I eat leeks?"

"You're so fond of nibbling," he said gaily, was silent for a second, then added tenderly, "You're so beautiful, Plana."

"Catch me," she called, and ran past him and away.

Instantly he bounded after her.

They rushed out on the meadow, one after the other, in a circle, as they had in their childhood days.

But it was no longer for the sake of the innocent sport itself, as it once had been. Their merriment had a deeper tinge now. They felt the spring, they felt the happiness of love.

Felix Salten

best known as the author of *Bambi,* the princely deer who appeared on the screen in Walt Disney's motion picture, was born in Budapest on September 6, 1869, and fled from Austria when Hitler invaded that country. He wrote the original story of *Bambi* before leaving Vienna, and wrote the book for the movie in Switzerland, where he died in exile in 1945.

Salten's childhood was poverty-stricken, and he himself was small and frail and bullied by his schoolmates. His youth was further embittered by the necessity of accepting charity from a cousin: he insisted that the cousin give him a job in his insurance office, and to compensate for the drudgery began to write stories. His relief came when several established writers became interested in the unhappy, talented boy and helped him to gain a place in literary magazines.

One of Salten's great idols was Emile Zola, and Salten became famous overnight through a brilliant obituary of the French novelist.

Perhaps the sorrows of his early life made him so keenly sympathetic with animals. He wrote both historical and contemporary novels, short stories, dramas and essays—nearly forty volumes in his lifetime—but in English he is known primarily as the creator of *Bambi* books, dear to both children and adults, which enter uncannily into the inner life of the forest animals. In addition to *Bambi* and *Fifteen Rabbits,* his other works include *Perri, The Hound of Florence, Florian, the Emperor's Stallion, Bambi's Children, Good Comrades,* and *The City Jungle.*

John Galsworthy admitted that he did not like the method "which places human words in the mouth of dumb creatures," yet he praised Salten because "behind the conversation, one feels the real sensations of the creatures who speak."